TRUELESBIANLOVE.COM

by

Carsen Taite

2008

TRUELESBIANLOVE.COM
© 2008 BY CARSEN TAITE. ALL RIGHTS RESERVED.

CREDITS
PRODUCTION DESIGN: STACIA SEAMAN
COVER DESIGN BY BOLD STROKES BOOKS GRAPHICS

Acknowledgments

I've spent years talking about my dream of becoming a writer. I used to say that one day when I find the time, I'm going to sit down and write a book. Endless thanks to my wife and the rest of my family for always believing, without a shred of evidence to support it, that the day would finally come.

This story was inspired by the strong and wonderful friendships I am lucky to have, my home city—the diverse and vibrant Big D, and my unwavering belief in true love.

Thanks to my first readers and friends who encouraged and critiqued my work in progress: Sherry, Christie, Barb, and Tony. A special thanks to Brenda Adcock for mentoring me through the creative process. Thanks also to Dr. Liland for his advice about the medical profession.

Radclyffe and Jennifer Knight—I am flattered, honored, and awestruck to be working with you and the rest of the BSB team. I can't imagine a more nurturing environment for a fledging writer to learn the craft. Thank you for taking a chance on me.

To my wife, Lainey, who put aside her volumes of nonfiction to read a romance, of all things. Nothing was more inspiring than not being able to write fast enough to satisfy your desire to find out what happened next.

Dedication

For Lainey—my true love

CHAPTER ONE

The soft weight of Shannon's arms drew Dylan closer. Her hands, palms flat, fingers reaching, slid along Dylan's hips. The heat emanating from her touch was palpable. Dylan arched her back as Shannon moved one hand upward to circle her aching breasts, coaxing her nipples into fine points of pleasure.

"Shannon," she gasped. "Why are you still dressed?"

Shannon looked up from the side of Dylan's neck, where she'd left a trail of sultry kisses. "I haven't a clue."

And with that less than profound statement, she yanked her shirt over her head and leaned into Dylan's waiting arms. Her taut breasts were irresistible, crushed hotly against Dylan's. She...

"Mackenzie? Mac, are you in there? I need to talk to you, right now."

Sighing, Mackenzie Lewis slammed shut the pages of *Lost Lives, Lost Loves*, undraped herself from the comfy sofa where she'd been planted for the last hour, and propelled herself toward the door. When you own the business, you jump when someone calls.

"What's the problem?" She addressed the man standing in the center of the small group assembled near a stack of crates outside her office.

"The Fresh Stuff produce delivery is all wrong, again," her frazzled chef said. "I can't keep overlooking their mistakes. I know you want to help them get started in business, but if this keeps happening, you won't have business to give them." He waved at the crates. "Four extra cases of tomatoes and not the right ones. I specifically ordered Heirloom and Roma. I can't work with Beefsteaks and I don't have time to cook them down into chutney we'll never use."

"Then perhaps we should wait until they spoil, so I can throw them at temperamental chefs who interrupt me with rants about produce." Mac glanced around at the other staff. "A tomato crisis is not a cause for everyone to abandon their posts. Scatter!" She instructed Nick, "Send the Beefsteaks to the Angel Network with ·my sincere apologies to all the homebound patients who depend on their delivered meals, for having to endure low-class tomatoes."

She couldn't help but smile at the pout planted firmly on his face. Blond, blue-eyed Nick Walters was a striking figure, making even his baggy chef pants look stylish. No wonder so many cute guys flocked to the Lakeside in hopes of catching a glimpse of him. Mac liked the balance he brought to the place. She wanted her patio bar and restaurant to be a comfortable spot for all members of the Dallas community. His ability to draw a crowd was worth a few fits now and then.

"Business is good and the Lakeside is doing fine," she assured him. "We can afford to donate a few cases of tomatoes."

"Fine, Mac, forgive me for trying to save you from your charitable business practices." Nick sighed dramatically. "If you don't mind, I'll do the next produce order myself. I have a reputation to protect, you know."

Mac nodded. "That's precisely why I hope you choose to stay in Big D, my friend. I want your reputation to be my reputation."

She knew when New Orleans eventually recovered from the ravages of Hurricane Katrina, there was a chance he would return to work in his hometown. By then, she hoped the thriving Dallas economy would encourage him to stay and rise to culinary stardom here.

Nick finally let a slow, full smile creep across his face. "I promise I won't leave until after we close the kitchen tonight."

As he made his way toward the kitchen doors, Mac glanced at her watch. Yes, she could grab another half hour curled up with *Lost Lives* before the evening shift arrived. She turned back toward her office and promptly stumbled into the arms of a gorgeous redhead. Startled, she stared at her best friend, Jordan Wagner. "Hey, Jordan. What's up?"

"The girls are on the Dock." Jordan referred to the covered back patio of the Lakeside. "We're checking out Batwoman. I had no idea you were already here."

Mac thought about the delicious chapter waiting on the other side of the office door. Her friends could wait. She wasn't quite ready to socialize. "Look, I'm on my way to the office to run some numbers. Order some food from the bar and I'll meet you girls back there in about an hour."

"It's the weekend. Numbers are for Mondays." Jordan grabbed Mac's hand and pulled her away from the office door. When Mac resisted, she cocked her head and eyed her suspiciously. "You look a little too anxious to get in there. I seriously doubt it's numbers you're crunching. Got a hot date waiting?"

"Didn't you say something about Batwoman?" Mac deflected.

Jordan shrugged. "Okay, I can take a hint." As she walked away, she added, "Let me know if you need any help."

Once back in her secure den of an office, Mac reached for her "hot date" and snuggled back onto her slipcovered sofa, flipping through pages to find her place. She felt a twinge of guilt for taking this small break from her day, not to mention leaving her friends to fend for themselves. Lowering the book, she glanced across her office, past the gravity bike rack where her two favorite rides awaited her, a frosty silver white Terry Isis road bike and a Trek Fuel EX 9 mountain bike. The adjoining wall was lined with shelf after shelf of lesbian romance novels, with a few mysteries sprinkled in here and there to keep her from looking like a total lesbian Harlequin junkie.

Obviously it wasn't healthy to prefer the company of imaginary characters in a book when she had friends waiting, so she vowed she would finish the next chapter and emerge before they gave up on her.

It had been an hour since their first touch, but Shannon was just as responsive at sunrise as she'd been at sunset. Dylan let her fingers drift over the hills and valleys open to her exploration. As the ample mountains of Shannon's chest moved, she moved also and began another ascent to ecstasy.

"What would you like me to do now, dear?" Dylan asked her new lover, knowing the list of unexplored possibilities was shorter now than it had been the night before.

"Well, darling, I want you to put one hand here." Shannon gently directed Dylan toward her left breast. "And, the other hand here." She gasped, motioning to her right breast. "And your lovely and talented tongue…"

The sharp ring of the office phone jerked Mac away from the pages. Closing the book for good, she reached for the phone, and snarled, "Hello?"

"Hello, yourself. Is that a demonstration of the fabulous hospitality one can expect at the Lakeside?"

Recognizing the voice of her friend Aimee, Mac softened her tone. "Sorry, I was trying to grab a few minutes, but that's apparently not possible."

"Jordan said you were in your office with some woman and we wanted to make sure you didn't need our help." Aimee let loose a slight snicker as she spoke.

Hearing more giggles in the background, Mac resigned herself to admiring the foxy lezzy superhero. "Fine, I'm on my way. How can I resist all this clamoring for my attention?"

She tucked *Lost Lives, Lost Loves* behind a cushion and made her way through the Lakeside Patio Bar & Grill, enjoying the touch of exhilaration she felt every time she realized this was her place. A walk through the restaurant was more than a walk, it was a patrol. Though she maintained a relaxed demeanor, her employees knew the Lakeside was her baby and that she expected a good explanation for any bumps and bruises that occurred while they took care of it. She swept a quick look around the tricked-out commercial kitchen, the heart of the restaurant. The shiny stainless surfaces were briefly immaculate in the interval before the dinner prep began. Nick was in the house and he had no tolerance for clutter.

She continued out into the restaurant, stopping at the stone and mosaic-tiled hostess stand located near the front doors. She'd used the work of local artisans in the design of the Lakeside, and this unique stand was a showpiece. The surrounding walls formed a mini-gallery that sported a rotating series of work by local artists. Sally Gannon, her restaurant manager, was near the stand, showing their newest hostess the ropes.

Mac paused to check in. "Need me for anything?"

Sally shook her head. She was a no-nonsense woman who'd worked at the Lakeside since the doors opened. "Looks like we're in good shape for tonight. Have some fun and don't worry about a thing. Will your friends want to stay for dinner?"

"No, we'll graze a little and then head out. Jordan and I have dates for the Resource Center fund-raiser later."

Mac left the bar, which was situated near the front of the restaurant, and strolled through the empty dining room to the covered back patio of the restaurant. In the late afternoon hours before dinnertime, most visitors to the Lakeside assembled on the Dock to enjoy a taste of the outdoors. The patio offered a fantastic view of White Rock Lake with the unique Dallas skyline looming large in the background. The temperate Dallas climate allowed the wood-framed glass doors that stood between the guests and the lake to stay open most of the year, and an abundance of ceiling fans kept things cool during summer's heat. The Dock was Mac's favorite room in the place. She and her friends spent many hours on this patio, kicking back in the comfortable sofas and chairs that were grouped as if in mini–living room settings. The reclaimed hardwood floors of the restaurant interior extended out onto the Dock, giving the outside room the same cozy feel as the interior.

Mac spotted her friends camped out as close to the open glass doors as possible, obviously enjoying this sunny Saturday afternoon. Jordan was leaning against the rail, looking on as Aimee Howard read aloud to the rest of the group from a magazine. Aimee owned a boutique real estate agency and had made herself wealthy selling homes in some of Dallas's most unique neighborhoods. They'd known each other since college, and it didn't surprise Mac to see her addressing the group as if she were holding court.

"Now, this is my dream girl," Aimee said. "What a total babe."

Sliding up behind her, Mac remarked, "Talking about me again?"

"Sweetie, you know I love you, but Kate Kane rocks my world."

"Who in the hell is Kate Kane, when did you met this dream girl, and more importantly, when do we get to meet her?" Mac demanded.

Aimee grinned and shook a comic under Mac's nose. "Finally, a lesbian superhero. Kate Kane is Batwoman. Tall, gorgeous, a red-haired spitfire. Millionaire socialite by day and sexy, powerful superhero by night." She fluttered her eyelashes. "That's something we have in common."

"Are we in time for an intervention?" Mac addressed the friends sitting around the table. "Or have we lost Aimee to the lures of the comic book girlfriend?"

She sometimes wondered if Aimee grew tired of being badgered about her serial monogamy. Aimee typified the U-Haul lesbian stereotype, except that her prospective soul mates were usually the ones doing the moving in and out of Aimee's spacious Lake Highlands residence. Mac was secretly happy that Aimee's travails distracted the group from their other favorite topic, her own depressing love life.

"Hey, I'm no worse than you," Aimee retorted. "Lusting over all those woman in books. At least I actually get out and date real women on occasion. Those who *live* in fantasy worlds shouldn't criticize those of us who make the occasional trip into reality."

"Ease up, girlfriend," Mac protested. "I date. I have a date tonight, in fact."

Her friends guffawed as Aimee taunted, "Another Jordan setup?"

"What if it is?" Mac tried not to sound defensive.

She couldn't remember the last real date she had been on. It was true that the last few times she had been out, it was on a double date with Jordan. Devastatingly good looks and a highly successful plastic surgery practice made Dr. Jordan Wagner one of the hottest tickets in town. Somehow the women she attracted always seemed to have a sidekick, and Jordan would entreat Mac to make up a foursome. Mac found the invitations convenient. It wasn't that she didn't want to be dating someone, or that she wasn't desirable herself, but it seemed like such a pain to get out and meet women. Frankly, she'd been on her own in the dating scene for so long, she wasn't even sure she knew where to start.

"Honey, you don't need Jordan to get you a date." Aimee sought to soften her taunting. "You could have anyone you wanted."

"Thanks for the vote of confidence." Mac glanced past Aimee to the newly married couple of their circle. Megan couldn't seem to stop hugging her wife, making the usually stoic Haley blush deep crimson. They appeared to be on cloud nine. It probably helped that they'd fallen in love with real women, not fictional superheroes like Kate Kane. She wasn't quite as fortunate. "Where are these legions of desirable women from whom I can have my pick? It's not like they're parading themselves by my house asking for a date."

"Yeah, well, you kind of have to give it some effort," Aimee said. "You know, put yourself out there where they can find you."

"Then you'll be happy to know what I'm doing tonight. I'm taking what is sure to be a beautiful woman to the Resource Center benefit, and maybe she'll be my soul mate."

"Oh, I'm sure she'll be beautiful," Aimee said. "But have any of Jordan's setups been soul-mate material so far?"

"Hold on there, matchmaker," Jordan objected. "What's this about a soul mate? Are you suggesting it's impossible to have a good time on a date unless you think she's a marriage prospect? In my experience, thoughts like that can kill an evening."

"Well, I will concede that your experience is vast," Aimee teased.

"Hey, I'm not ashamed of the fact I put myself out there. In my line of work, I think it's important to be an ardent observer of the human form." Jordan illustrated her point by drawing curves in the air with both hands.

"Sure, Dr. Wagner, you can call your serial dating 'research.' But we all know you're only interested in one thing, and once you get it, you move on to the next 'experiment.'"

"Ouch. It's a dirty job."

"Enough, you two." Mac interrupted the friendly sparring and playfully pushed her best friends apart.

"Break it up, ladies," Nick called as he approached. "Your food is here and I won't have your fighting ruin the presentation."

Aimee glanced longingly at the platters of scrumptious-looking appetizers. "Don't worry, the only fighting we'll be doing from here on out is over the last morsel."

Turning to Mac, Nick said, "Sorry to disturb the festivities, but your assistance is needed in the bar, something to do with beer, ice, and not enough glasses."

"Don't wait on me, girls. There's no telling how long I'll be." Mac grabbed a crab cake off the nearest platter. "Jordan, are you picking me up tonight?"

"Yes, see you at your place at seven."

As she walked away, Mac heard Aimee ask, "Who's Mac's date? Is she hot?"

"A ten out of ten, and *very* willing," Jordan replied. "If Mac doesn't score with *her*, we'd better start thinking about an intervention."

Chapter Two

L acy Holmes was definitely a ten, leggy and gorgeous, an international flight attendant with raven hair and deep blue eyes that created the perfect contrast for her fair skin. She had a beautiful smile that dazzled all who glanced her way, and she was sending all the right signals. Yet, looking at her, Mac felt nothing.

"Would you like to dance?" Lacy whispered in her ear.

The music was Queen, not exactly groovin', but dancing seemed like a good way to avoid the complete disintegration of their conversation. Lacy was nice enough, but so far all she'd wanted to talk about was shopping or dining out. Current events and politics either didn't interest her or were outside her repertoire. Mac couldn't tell which and wasn't sure if she cared enough to figure it out.

She offered her hand to Lacy. "Sure, let's dance."

As they reached the dance floor, the music changed to a slow, swaying tune. Lacy clasped her hands around Mac's waist and eased in close as they moved together. Mac let herself relax and follow Lacy's lead, musing to herself how much easier it was to lose herself in the music than in the woman she was holding. Beyoncé's "Naughty Girl" blared from the speakers. Noting the song sampled "Love to Love You Baby" by Donna

Summer, Mac smiled. Retro music was the best music, she concluded, letting her gaze trawl the room.

The place was packed with politicians, socialites, and well-heeled members of the Dallas gay and lesbian community. She caught sight of Jordan and her date, heads together and seemingly deep in conversation. Her mind flashed through a collection of high school dance memories. In those scenes she was the one with Jordan, leaning close to exchange deep teenage revelations while their dates sat idly by, dreaming of more intimate acts that would never happen. The music was pretty much the same back then as it was tonight. Now, every time she heard a song by the Bangles, Janet Jackson, or Gloria Estefan, memories of good times shared with Jordan sprang to mind.

From the moment they'd met, she'd known they would always be friends. Jordan's beauty drew her in, but her steadfast loyalty won Mac's heart and they'd been inseparable for years. She glanced again at her best friend and wondered what in the world she had in common with her willowy brunette date. Other than beauty, Mac could think of nothing. The woman was a model, so Mac couldn't imagine she shared the same types of experiences as Jordan, certainly not enough to craft a deep and meaningful conversation. They looked fantastic together, almost a perfect match. The brunette wore a slinky black gown and Jordan was elegant in a jet-black Armani suit and Manolo Blahnik sling-back sandals pushing her well over the six-foot mark. They were probably talking about how many times and places they were going to do it when they left here tonight, Mac decided.

As if reading her mind, Lacy angled in for a kiss. Lost in the sway of the dance, Mac met her lips. The kiss was light, smooth, and nice. Well, thought Mac, maybe she and Lacy could talk about how many times and places they would do it when they left the party. She kissed her date again, lingering this time. Another nice kiss, but not a firework in sight. She persevered and Lacy responded in kind, her lips locking on and her breasts rising and falling more heavily against Mac's. Their tongues slid together just enough to make Mac realize her mouth was dry, like the rest of her. There was nothing wrong with Lacy's technique, and her breath was minty, but nice wasn't enough to spur a night of passion.

Mac began to ease out of her grasp, but Lacy wasn't letting go. Leaning her head back to expose more of her throat, she gazed into Mac's eyes and asked, "Want to take me home?"

Mac paused for a long moment, knowing she would be one of the few to decline such an offer from the beautiful Ms. Lacy Holmes. Then she burst into a big, wide yawn she couldn't hide. "Actually, I'm very tired and I have to be at the restaurant early in the morning. Would you mind terribly if we left now?"

Mac could tell that Lacy was disappointed at the abrupt announcement that the evening was coming to an end. Her hand moved slowly down Mac's hip. Her stare become inviting. She made it clear that she had a different take on Mac's request. "An early night wasn't what I had in mind, but you're right. Why wait until we're running out of energy?"

Mac wavered for an instant, attempting to reason with herself. Maybe she was having some kind of confidence crisis and her reluctance would instantly vanish once she got Lacy home and they were alone. The perfect solution to a libido deficit was standing right in front of her. This gorgeous woman probably had flings in every layover city, so there would be no complications if they didn't call each other the next day. Mac didn't have to marry her. What was the problem?

Puzzled and rather embarrassed by her lack of interest, she said something noncommittal and guided Lacy back to the table. Jordan was so engrossed in her glamorous date, she didn't notice them until Mac cleared her throat noisily and asked, "Jordan, are you about ready to go? I have an early morning tomorrow."

Jordan, eyes still on the brunette, replied, "Sure you do, Mac. Don't you mean you want to get started on a late night, tonight?"

Mac stifled a sigh. Jordan was the designated driver, otherwise they wouldn't have to have this conversation. She knew she should have brought her own car. "Jordan, if you're not ready to leave, I'll get a cab."

The sharpness in her tone grabbed Jordan's attention and she eased out of her chair telling her date, "I'm going to go collect our silent auction winnings with Mac. We'll be right back." She grabbed Mac's arm and propelled her to the edge of the ballroom, leaving the other women staring after them. "Why do you want to go? I thought you were having a good time."

"I've had a great time, but it's late and I have to help with the new menu tasting tomorrow."

"What about Lacy? She looks like she wants to spend more time with you."

"Lacy's fine, but I don't want to sleep with her. I want to go home. Alone."

"Okay, I'll take you. It's impossible to get a cab in Dallas."

"Thank you. I promise I'll only cramp your style for the short time it'll take to drive me home."

Jordan gave her an odd look. "I'm not worried about that. Look, I'm sorry you're not enjoying yourself. I thought the two of you would hit it off."

"Why, Jordan? Because we're both the same height?" Mac snapped. Catching herself, she backed off. "I'm sorry.

I'm tired. I'll admit she is gorgeous, but somewhat lacking in the depth department. Pretty is nice, but it doesn't top the list of things I am looking for in a lover. I need someone I can talk to about more than the latest shoe sale at Nordstrom."

Jordan gave her a conciliatory hug. "Why, dear, you have me for that."

❖

"If I were you, I would sell my house and live here on the Dock." Aimee leaned her head back and took in a lungful of the crisp air skimming across the lake. She folded the Sunday newspaper she'd been skimming and placed it on the table beside her. "Nick could make all the wonderful snacks you'd need and you could have one of the cuties here wait on you hand and foot. Every once in a while you could hook up with a well-sculpted cyclist fresh off the trail and looking for a little refreshment, if you know what I mean."

Mac closed her book. "Yeah, maybe I should take that advice. I could loaf around out here and still stay connected to the outside world." She leaned back on the cushioned deck chair and crossed her legs. "We're offering free wireless for customers now."

"Not before time," Aimee said. "I spend half my life on blogs. You could even post a site-of-the-day on the specials board for the folks who want to use the Internet for its intended purpose—fun."

"What kind of fun are we discussing today?" a voice called from the trail that ran below the deck, and Jordan approached, obviously fresh from a ride. Her hair was slightly mussed and she wore bike shorts, a Pearl Izumi jersey, and cleated Sidi cycling shoes. She locked her bike on the rack at the edge of the deck before striding up to the Dock.

"Speaking of well-sculpted cyclists, look who decided to join us instead of bathing." Aimee scooted way over on the lounger as if to give Jordan plenty of space as she passed by.

"I carry the scent of good health," Jordan said, sliding her fingers back through her copper waves. "Thirty miles and I was barely warmed up when I realized what time it was. Thought I better head on over here before Mac fed my brunch to the birds. What kind of fun are we discussing?"

"Mac's joined the modern age and installed Wi-Fi at the restaurant," Aimee said.

"That's terrific." Jordan settled herself on the lounger only inches from Aimee, who waved her away while pinching her nose. "Mind if I check my e-mail while we wait on brunch? I want to send a quick thank-you to my lovely date for last night. She was asleep when I left this morning."

"I can't believe you had the energy to ride thirty miles this morning after playing the ardent lover all night," Mac remarked. Actually, she was surprised at how great Jordan looked after a night of physical activity followed by a morning of more of the same. Her sleeveless jersey and tight bike shorts showed off every well-formed muscle, and her toned and tanned body glowed from her exertions.

"Can't you call her on the phone like normal women do the morning after?" Aimee asked.

"E-mail is definitely not romantic," Mac added.

"We can't all be as romantic as the main characters in your beloved romance novels," Jordan replied casually. "And after the night we had, she's probably still sleeping. It wouldn't be very charming of me to wake her with the abrupt ringing of a phone. If I send her an e-mail, she can read it and respond at her leisure. Also, most importantly, I can be short and to the point."

"Translation…" Mac mused aloud. "You won't get put on the spot with questions like 'when will I see you again?'"

Before Jordan could respond, Aimee chimed in, "I don't see what's wrong with a morning-after e-mail instead of the obligatory phone call. Look at how many online dating sites there are out there. Web sites are replacing bars and e-mail is replacing phone calls. Everything is virtual."

"Sounds like a great way to meet the woman of one's dreams," Mac said with irony. "I could just sit around at home in my pj's and 'date' online."

Jordan interjected, "Now, wait a minute. I think e-mail's great, but it's no substitute for real-life encounters. I need to see what I'm getting myself into before I invest my time."

"Yeah, you wouldn't want to throw away a whole evening finding out what someone thought or who they were," Aimee retorted. "Don't you ever wonder what it would be like to spend time actually chatting with your conquests without physical distractions."

"I'm not distracted by things physical, they're the focus. It's all the chatting that can make me lose interest."

"Don't listen to her," Aimee told Mac. "She may be hopeless, but you don't have to be. Sign up on one of the dating sites. You never know, you might meet someone special."

"Mac had a beautiful woman right in her arms last night and still went home alone," Jordan remarked. "Do you seriously think it's going to be easier for her to find the perfect mate?"

"She was beautiful," Mac admitted. "But we had nothing in common. I'm looking for more in a relationship."

"I had no idea you were so serious about finding Ms. Right."

Slightly annoyed, Mac said, "You're so busy fixing me up with one-night stands, you haven't been listening."

"Well, forgive me for trying to find someone you'd be interested in."

"What about you, Jordan?" Aimee ignored their bickering. "Your hunt-and-gather method doesn't seem to be working for Mac. Have you had more luck?"

"I'm not complaining," Jordan replied. "I have fun."

"That's not what I'm asking."

"Jordan isn't looking for true love," Mac said, earning a sharp stare from her best friend.

"Sure, it's enough to have us adoring her." Aimee fluttered her eyelashes.

Laughing, Jordan said, "I've never said I don't want a long-term relationship...sometime."

"I have an idea." Aimee grinned. "Why don't you both look online? Let's see who meets someone special first."

When Jordan hesitated, Mac said, "I'll do it if you will. We can compare notes. I bet you dinner, prepared by the winner, you make a date before I do."

Jordan gave a resigned shrug. "Can't pass up that bet. When do we start?"

CHAPTER THREE

"Truelesbianlove dot com?" Mac studied the screen Aimee had gleefully opened.

"That's ambitious marketing," Jordan noted. "Who's going to find true love on a Web site?"

"Ignore her, Mac. The World Wide Web is big enough for both of you to find what you're looking for." Aimee situated the laptop where they could all see the screen. "Read some of the profiles before you try writing one. Maybe you'll even see someone interesting you can reply to."

Jordan took over and began scrolling through the listings of women seeking women in the Dallas area. "I can tell already that poor spelling and grammar are going to drive Mac crazy." She chuckled as she looked through the list. "Of course, that leaves plenty more women for me, since I'm willing to overlook improper use of apostrophes if everything else is up to standard."

"What you're saying is, if the woman's a babe, then it doesn't matter if she can't write her way out of a paper bag," Mac retorted. "Fine, you can have all the women who didn't bother to post a picture since your standards don't include looks."

"Oh, now you're making fun of me because I have standards other than 'how does she look in a swimsuit?'"

"Sounds like this is going well." A hand landed on Mac's shoulder and Megan leaned over her to inspect the screen.

"Sorry we're late," Haley said, pulling up another chair. "What are y'all doing?"

"We thought for sure you would have started eating without us," Megan added. "Haley worked night shift, so it took us a while to get here."

"No problem," Mac said. Haley was a paramedic for the Dallas Fire Department and often spent her weekends on long, stressful shifts dealing with the chaos big-city life could dish out.

Aimee waved to the couple, "We're researching the world of online dating. Jordan and Mac need to spread the net wider."

"Don't tell me you've finally exhausted your dating pool." Megan elbowed Jordan playfully.

"Yes, I've spent at least one night with every available woman in Dallas. Now I need the power of the Internet to help me locate and satisfy the remaining few." Jordan rolled her eyes at the ensuing silence. "I'm kidding, people. Hell, you really do think I am a shallow sex fiend."

Megan hugged her tightly. "No, we don't, sweetie. I think you truly like all the women you date, but you talk about your conquests like they don't matter. I sometimes wonder why you minimize your feelings about them. Is it because you're intent on appearing to dodge the commitments of a relationship?"

"Ah, spoken like a true psychotherapist. Save it for the paying customers, sister."

Megan was a psychologist in private practice. She and Jordan had a professional relationship that had blossomed into a friendship, bringing Megan and Haley into Mac's circle.

Megan's tendency to analyze everyone was a running joke among the friends, and she took their teasing in good humor.

"Are you telling me I'm way off base?" Megan asked Jordan.

"I like women, lots of them. My penchant for variety precludes a relationship like the one you have."

Megan grinned. "You mean married bliss?"

"Let's just say I don't need all the warm fuzzies you relationship lovers seem to crave. Walks in the rain, sharing coffee over the morning paper, leaning arm in arm over the balcony to watch a beautiful sunset. Don't get me wrong, I like romance, but I see myself doing all of those things with many different women for the rest of my life, not the same one, day after day. At least I'm honest about what I want."

"Well, that kind of honesty isn't going to net you many responses online," Haley chimed in. "Most of the profiles here are from women looking to find that special someone."

"I bet a lot of them want exactly what I do, but they don't think it's PC to admit it," Jordan said. "They'll come out of the woodwork when they see they're not alone. I'm going to write an honest profile. Maybe I'll start a trend."

"Yeah, yeah, whatever." Mac moved closer to the computer. "Can we see what's out there now so I can start wading in the world wide dating pool?"

Aimee began typing. "Let's start with age range. Thirty to thirty-five, within twenty-five miles of Dallas…"

Mac stopped her. "Twenty-five miles! That could mean two hours in bad traffic. Make it ten."

"You can always narrow the search later, but if it's not broad enough to begin with, you may not get many results."

"Great, what happens when she falls in love with the profile of a woman who lives too far away for convenient dating?" Haley commented.

"She'll either get over it or decide not to let silly things like distance interfere with true love." As she typed, Aimee asked, "Is anyone else hungry?"

"Don't worry," Mac replied. "Nick's about to parade out the entire new menu for you to sample. Do we have any matches yet?"

"Here you go. Eighteen women waiting for you to lavish them with your affection. All but three have pictures."

Jordan leaned in. "Delete those three. Seriously, Mac, it's not a matter of looks versus personality. The fact that they don't have a picture should tell you something about their sense of security with their appearance."

"Maybe they don't want the whole world to know they're trawling for dates on an online site," Mac said.

"Then they should find another way to meet people. I say if you are going to put yourself out there, do it all the way."

"First up, LuvintheCity. She's five-five, slender build, auburn hair. Lives with a roommate, college degree…"

Mac groaned. "Her picture's not bad, but I have this phobia about people who feel the need to alter the spelling of words to be cute. Luv? Now isn't that cute?"

"Fine, no cute spellings." Aimee gestured at the monitor. "Which rules out almost all these profiles. Shall I just close the search down, Mac, or can you get over it?"

"Is that a prom dress?" Jordan pointed at a picture before Mac could reply. "And who is that woman in the other picture with her? Looks like they're about to rip each other's clothes off."

Megan joined in. "What's the point of a pic like that? Is she trying to prove she's been found attractive by at least one other female? 'This woman thinks I am beautiful and you should too. Text me now!'"

"Check this one out." Jordan pointed at another thumbnail pic. "Is that a mullet?"

Aimee clapped her hands together. "Ladies, please. We could sit here all day making fun of other people's profiles, but if you want to start meeting some women, you need to start writing your own. First you need a handle. Pick something short and catchy that conveys who you are or what you're looking for."

"Handle?" Mac frowned. "It's not like we're truckers looking for love on our CB radios."

"So, are you saying you want me to put your real name online?" Aimee asked sarcastically. "And maybe your social security number too, so that you can't possibly be accused of hiding behind a user ID?"

Jordan laughed. "I have the perfect handle for myself. 'Skin Deep.'"

Aimee tsked. "Is that really the message you want to convey?"

"Absolutely. Type it up, Ms. Howard."

Aimee glanced at Mac. "Who are you going to be? Please pick something a little more subtle than our doctor friend."

"How about 'Laker Gal'?"

"Okay, there are some basic questions to whip through. You're both out lesbians, not bi. You live alone. You're single, never been married, no kids. Do either of you want kids?"

"I thought that was the beauty of being lesbian." Mac replied. "We don't have to have to prove ourselves by having children."

"Well spoken," Jordan said.

"I'll take that as a no to the kid question." Aimee continued to type. "Now, let's talk about physical appearance. We have a drop-down menu for overall looks. Here are your choices.

'People whistle when I walk by. All my other girlfriends thought I looked good. I clean-up real well.' Or, 'My mother thinks I am adorable.' Which is it, girls?"

"Hell, I don't know," Mac said. "I do clean up okay and I guess I am reasonably attractive."

Jordan punched her in the arm. "Who are you kidding? People definitely whistle, if they can pick their tongues up off the floor, when you walk by. You're gorgeous."

Mac blushed. "Well, coming from Dallas's premier connoisseur of good looks, that's quite a compliment."

Looking closely at her best friend, Jordan thought indeed Mac was a looker. Certainly, this wasn't a new realization, but it had been a long time since she'd thought objectively about Mac's beauty. She was somewhere around five-six or five-seven. Her cyclist body boasted a lean, athletic build cut in all the right places. Her thick, blond hair was cut in a sassy, short style that Mac wore slightly spiked. Her face glowed from sun and outdoor exercise. Honey brown eyes reflected her love of life and laughter. Yes, she was definitely likely to draw compliments from passersby, whistles included.

"Aimee, check the 'people whistle' comment for both of us," Jordan ordered. Turning back to Mac, she explained, "You may as well show confidence. It's more attractive than modesty."

"Fine," Aimee said. "Now you have to write something about yourself and what you're looking for, in your own words." She turned the laptop toward Jordan. "You go first. Something tells me you already know exactly what you want to say."

As Jordan typed, the rest of the group congregated at the far end of the Dock to allow her to write uninterrupted. She didn't spend a lot of time thinking about what she was writing. The words flowed easily from a store of life experience. This little online adventure would only serve one purpose for her, and that was to demonstrate that deep romantic relationships were nothing more than a sham. No matter what people said about true love and undying commitment, staying power was only as strong as the depth of physical desire. Life's lessons had made that truth clear, and Jordan lived by the principle that true love didn't exist.

She stopped typing and reviewed her missive:

Skin Deep's Message to Prospective Matches:

Who are we kidding? Basic physical attraction is the foundation of all intimate relationships. If my picture on this site doesn't get you going, you're not going to contact me, no matter what I say about myself. I will tell you this: What you see is what you get, and I expect the same. I promise if you live up to your end of the bargain, we can have a date that fulfills even the most spectacular expectations. My motto is: anything goes. If you're looking for true love and forever after, I am not for you. I won't tie you up, not with relationship strings anyway, and either one of us can decide when enough is enough.

Jordan paused before saving her work. She could imagine what the group would say, but she didn't get why everyone thought it was mandatory to pair off into happy couples, especially when it was clear that there was no such thing. Relationships didn't last, no matter how hard couples tried. With a slight pang, she glanced at the newly married Megan and Haley, then hit the Save button and announced, "I'm done."

"Well, that took all of two minutes." Aimee paused

between bites of a thin crust pizza. "Let's see what all the online babes are going to learn about you."

"It won't take long." Jordan slid the laptop across the table and picked up a plate. The food looked delicious.

As she made her selections, Aimee read Skin Deep's brief philosophy on love and romance aloud, punctuating the sharp words with disparaging facial expressions. By the time she finished reading, her face was scrunched into wrinkles of disbelief. "Is this the best you could do? Couldn't you at least act like you're trying to meet someone?"

"Why should I?" Jordan sliced into a delicate phyllo pastry triangle. "You started this little experiment and I'm only participating so I can prove my theory that not everyone online is looking for love. I'm sure lots of women are scared to admit their innermost desires in case their friends think they're shallow. You gals already think I am shallow, so I have nothing to lose. I'm using my shallowness to flush out the rest of the fun-loving woman on the Web."

"You're hopeless." Aimee moved the computer in Mac's direction. "Ready?"

"Sure, why not. But I may need more than the two minutes Jordan took."

As her friends ate and chatted, Mac stared blankly at the computer screen, willing inspiration to take over. God knew, she didn't share her best friend's philosophy. Jordan's cynical take on love was distasteful, yet Mac wasn't sure whether she could articulate her own. She wasn't completely certain what she believed about love and the path toward it. She'd had a good example of true love while growing up. Her parents couldn't have been more perfect for one another, and their every action demonstrated their deep commitment and undying love. They'd first met in college when their eyes locked across a crowded room. According to her mother, time had stopped and no one else existed in that magic moment. The story had always seemed so clichéd, but cliché or not, their love was proof that romance wasn't dead. She should be so lucky to find something even close to what they had.

Concentrating, she typed:

Laker Gal seeks deep waters.
I'm a successful entrepreneur and, like most business owners, I've spent years being wed to my work. It's time for me to find a new relationship. My interests are diverse and surely some will intersect with yours. I love road and mountain cycling, romance novels, and great food. Where our interests diverge, perhaps we can each learn to love new things.
I, like you, believe in forever. We may not fall in love at first sight, but from our first glance we'll know there's a spark to be kindled. The feeling will be empowering, igniting us to fan the flame. We'll burn only for each other. There will be challenges to overcome. Winds of change will threaten to extinguish what we've built and we'll have to learn to feed the fire. No matter what, we will always remember how our love began, and nothing will quell the heat of our passion and commitment to each other.
If you want what I want, let's meet and see if there's a spark. Perhaps we'll start a fire that will burn forever.

As she read the words for the third time, Mac reflected that she was indeed a true romantic. She knew Jordan would poke fun, and that confirmed her belief that the message was exactly right, the very antithesis of Jordan's invitation for a quickie.

"All right, gang," she said. "Want to know how I'm going to attract my future wife?"

Her ears burned as she read aloud her declaration to the unknown future love interest. Only when she finished and her friends started clapping did she start to shake her embarrassment at having bared her feelings. Turning from her fans, she caught Jordan looking off into space with a strange expression on her face. Her features quickly spread into a wide grin when she met Mac's eyes.

"You think that's going to find you everlasting love?" There was a faint edge to her voice.

Mac shrugged. "I have nothing to lose."

"Except your illusions." Jordan gave her a pitying smile. "Are you really sure you want to do this?"

"Absolutely."

"Then let's post these and prepare to fend off the women." Jordan ate a dip-smeared carrot stick and slowly licked the residue off her fingers.

CHAPTER FOUR

W hat a crazy week," Mac sighed as she kicked off her shoes and flopped onto her living room sofa.

She usually worked only weekdays, but Sally Gannon had been out of town for the weekend on a trip planned well before the blistering heat wave showed up on the weather map. The oppressive temperatures sent Dallas residents packing from their own hot kitchens to flock into the cool, carefree dining at the Lakeside. Mac didn't feel confident enough to leave their less experienced assistant manager alone with the large crowds, so she'd worked from open to close both Saturday and Sunday. Though thankful for the business, she was glad that the week was over and that Sally would be back at the helm starting Monday morning.

She planned to do nothing but lie around in her boxers for the next two days. Maybe she would force herself out the door to see Jordan. The leisurely brunch a week earlier felt like a distant memory, and she hadn't heard from Jordan since. She could imagine why. Jordan was probably trying to keep up with e-mail from the online dating venture. Mac got off the sofa and went into the kitchen in search of a glass of wine. The room had been redesigned when she renovated the house several years earlier. Copper pots and pans secured on ceiling hooks complemented a Viking range and wall oven. Around the walls, plentiful cabinets showcased a collection of colorful Fiesta dinnerware and shiny Riedel barware.

Mac plucked a wineglass from one of the cabinets and took a bottle of Santa Margherita from the countertop wine cooler. She poured a healthy dose of the Pinot Grigio and switched on her Bose sound system. The latest Indigo Girls CD cranked up and filled the room with earthy harmonies. Mac sat at the rough-hewn wooden table, sipping from the cool glass and contemplating the blinking lights on her laptop computer. She hadn't read her personal e-mail all week but knew she had messages. She wasn't sure why she'd put off opening them. Yes, she'd been busy dealing with business matters, but not *that* busy. And it wasn't as if they'd know she had flour in her hair and raspberry sauce all over her shirt as she read the replies.

Flipping open the lid, she watched the screen come to life. At first she'd been leery about providing her personal e-mail account details to the dating site, imagining spam problems and even the occasional e-stalker. But truelesbianlove.com used a blind system so no one received her e-mail address. It was totally up to her whether she gave it out once she got to know someone.

She signed on and quickly scanned her messages before dealing with a couple of routine communications. All the while she was aware of the truelesbianlove.com replies lying in wait for her like landmines. Unsure of what she was about to trigger, she considered deleting all of them and removing her profile. Was it wise to invite fate into her orderly life? She took a deep breath and decided to find out.

Dear Laker Gal,
I like your name. I guess from your profile

that you live near one of the many lakes that surround Dallas. I do too, and I love it. I'm an avid fisherwoman and spend all my free time out on my boat trying to catch the big one. I'm looking for a woman who is not afraid of the sun, baiting her own hooks, or scaling her catch. Cooking it up, on the other hand, is a duty that we can both share. How about it? Are you up for some fishing that's not online?

    Hope to hear from you soon,
    Lookin4theBigOne

Mac laughed out loud. Did Lookin4theBigOne even read her profile in full before she expressed an interest? Mac clicked on the link that brought up her admirer's profile. There were several photographs of a trim, athletic young butch standing in various poses designed to demonstrate that she was handy with a boat and fishing equipment. Okay, she wasn't bad looking, but Mac's idea of a good time did not involve putting worms and bugs on hooks and then sitting around for hours waiting for the "big one" to come along. She started to delete the e-mail, but paused. She wasn't interested in fishing, but they might have other interests in common. Maybe she should at least write back and find out. But what if fishing was this woman's only interest? Mac would sooner be poked in the head with sharp sticks than have to listen to fish tales.

The phone rang as she deliberated, sparing her from having to make a decision. She answered and was relieved to hear her older brother Marty's voice.

"Hey, Mac. How're you doing?"

"Lying around living the life of the rich and famous," she joked.

"I figured as much. I always told you the restaurant

business would lead to a life of luxury. How in the world do you manage to fill your days?" Marty teased back.

They both knew better. Their parents had run a popular East Dallas diner for years. Mac and Marty, along with their brothers, had spent many hours after school and on weekends waiting tables, washing dishes, and doing prep work in the kitchen. After college, their brothers had sworn they would never darken the door of a restaurant again unless they had a reservation, but Mac had loved every minute of the experience. After getting her business degree from the University of Texas, she returned to East Dallas to manage the diner as her parents eased into retirement.

She was devastated when they were killed in a car wreck before they could ever do all they'd envisioned. Their sudden death made the good memories of the work they had shared too painful, and Mac had felt the four walls of the diner closing in. She'd sold the business and bought the property that soon became the Lakeside Patio Bar & Grill. Pouring her grief into the new venture, she found solace in carrying on her parents' tradition, hosting Dallasites looking for great food in a great atmosphere.

"What can I do for you, dear brother?" she asked.

"Alice wanted me to check if you're coming to Jeremy's birthday party?"

Mac recalled an invitation her sister-in-law had sent through the mail. She'd forgotten to reply. "Saturday after next, right?"

"Yep. We've rented a bounce house and we're doing a backyard barbeque. You don't have to cook, serve, or wash dishes, I swear."

"I'd love to come," Mac said. "You know I always make my appearances as the favorite aunt. What should I get him?"

"Anything to do with Spider-Man is a good bet. I'm glad you can make it. We haven't seen you in a while."

"I know. It's summer." She knew she didn't have to explain the busiest period of the year to her brother.

"Feel free to bring someone if you want," he said. "Are you seeing anyone?"

"Subtle, Marty. No, I'm not seeing anyone. I might bring Jordan if that's okay. I think she's been going through a little family withdrawal lately."

Jordan was virtually alone and had depended on the Lewis family ever since high school, when her mother had fought a long battle with cancer. Mac recalled the many late nights she'd held her distraught friend while Mrs. Wagner lay in the next room with hospice workers easing her into acceptance of the certainty of death. In between the long, draining visits at her mother's bedside, Jordan had spent hours at home with Mac.

Life in the Lewis household was busy but laid back, and Mac's parents made a point of making their children's friends feel at home. As a result, the place was always full of teenagers. Mac knew Jordan saw the Lewises as her second set of parents and their home as hers, also. The pattern continued through college, with Jordan spending many weekends with her, doing laundry and eating home-cooked meals.

Years of familiarity allowed Mac to read her best friend's thoughts. She could sense when Jordan was replaying the loss, not only of her own mother, but of Mac's parents as well. Mac thought a day with the Lewis family was in order.

"Bring her along," Marty said. "I was only wondering if there was anyone special yet."

"Well, to be honest, I am kind of looking, but it's a slow process."

"If you're looking within the four walls of the Lakeside, I bet it's slow. You should get out more."

"I suppose you think you're the first one to deliver that sage advice. Not to worry, big brother, I've expanded my search to the Internet. Aimee talked me into signing up with one of those online dating sites. In fact, I was reading a message from a potential prospect when you called."

"Well, when you finally decide to put yourself out there, you certainly go all the way. How's the prospect? Why don't you bring her along to the party?"

"Jeez, Marty, we haven't even met. I don't even know if I'm going to write her back. She spends all her free time fishing, from what I can tell. I can't picture myself baiting hooks and cleaning fish."

"Are you going to sit around and wait for Ms. Right to come along, or are you answering ads too?"

"Don't hassle me. I barely started this little venture."

"True love doesn't happen on its own, sis. Sometimes you have to go looking for it. Sometimes you even have to fight for it."

Mac was curious about the conviction her brother expressed, but she brushed it off. "When it's right, it will happen. Look at Mom and Dad. They weren't looking for true love, but they found it the very first time they laid eyes on each other."

"They loved each other, that's for sure. But that story about how they met didn't include all the complicating factors." Marty's voice tightened slightly. "Couples are often nostalgic about their first encounter. They want it to conform to the love-at-first-sight fantasy we all like to believe in. But the truth is, falling in love can be a messy process. As for staying in love, there are lots of bumps and bruises along the way."

"Who *are* you?" Mac asked in amazement. "That doesn't

even sound like something you'd say. Have you been watching Oprah? Since when did you become wise in the ways of love?"

After a beat of silence, Marty replied quietly, "Since Alice and I spent the last year seeing a marriage counselor."

Mac gasped. "What the hell? I thought you guys were madly in love and crazy about each other."

"We were. We are. But mad and crazy aren't always enough to get you through. All that passion at the beginning quickly fades when you have to find a way to blend your lives. You have to figure out where the lines are drawn. Trust me, if you don't do the work of compromise at the beginning, you'll have to do it eventually. There's no getting around it."

Mac thought about the stress Marty and Alice had gone through trying to have a baby. Their attempts at parenthood had obviously strained their relationship. "Well, you sure know how to get a girl all revved up about dating."

"I'm sorry. I want you to meet that perfect someone. But I guess I'm trying to say that perfection is a relative state, and it may require some work on your part to achieve it. Give some of these women a chance. You could be missing out because things don't look perfect from the get-go."

"Okay, old man, I'll try to learn from your experience. I still think I'm going to toss the fisherwoman back, though."

"Understood. See you at the party?"

"Spidey and I will be there." As Mac hung up the phone, she resolved to reply to at least some of the e-mails awaiting her. She turned back to her laptop and clicked on the next one. Someone who called herself NoNonsense wrote:

You have an interesting profile. Perhaps we should meet. I think we have a lot in common. I like books too. Let me know if you're interested.

Certainly short and to the point. Mac tried to see past the choppy, uninformative sentences to the woman who'd reached out to her. There was only one way. She typed a reply:

> Thanks for your e-mail. Glad to hear you're a booklover too. I find it's hard to balance all my life's loves: books, bicycling, and running a restaurant, but I do my best to give them all equal time. What are your other passions and how do you make the most of your time?

There, she said to herself, nothing like a question to get the conversation going.

"Eight messages. Pretty good for not even trying," Jordan remarked to herself.

She sat her laptop on the stainless steel countertop of the kitchen island and opened the fridge in search of a snack. Hours ago, she'd eaten something unrecognizable for dinner at the hospital where she'd spent the day on call, and she was desperate for some real food. Not that she expected to find any in her barren refrigerator. Neat rows of Fiji bottled water, a lone jar of apricot preserves, and a foil-wrapped swan containing aged leftovers stared back at her, mocking her hunger. Thank God for delivery, she thought, hitting the speed dial for her favorite Thai restaurant. She ordered the usual, tom kha gai soup and pad kee mao, extra spicy. Her next stop was the built-in bar, where she poured herself three fingers of Glenmorangie. Settling into a bar stool at the kitchen island, she sipped the mellow single-malt whisky and glanced around, automatically checking that everything was in order in her environment.

Her loft occupied the entire top floor of the old railway building in Deep Ellum, a neighborhood only blocks away from downtown Dallas. The exterior of the building retained its rustic warehouse look, while the interior was entirely modern with the exception of the old-fashioned screened-in elevator and the sliding steel doors that provided access to her apartment. Her sprawling living space had high ceilings and maple wood floors, and one of the reasons she'd bought the place was the enormous travertine-tiled bathroom. Most people would probably think six showerheads at various heights and angles was over the top, but bathing was a form of relaxation Jordan cherished. There was nothing like a massaging shower or a long soak in her whirlpool bathtub after a stress-filled day with her patients.

To the casual observer, the loft would probably look like a model home, showing few signs of an occupant. Jordan had chosen Danish furnishings and museum-quality modern artworks to enhance the sleek look of the living areas. Her clothes and personal items were tucked away in cubbies customized to her preferences. She didn't like clutter; her work delivered all the chaos she could handle. The loft was her retreat, a tranquil zone where she could renew herself and escape from the demands of others.

Turning to her computer, she inspected her latest messages. More of the same, no doubt. She'd spent the past week deleting offers from women who seemed to think she was only kidding about wanting a casual hook-up, or that she was damaged goods hiding her true yearnings behind a shield of flippancy. It was incredible, she thought, how complete strangers thought they could analyze someone from a few sentences on an Internet dating site. She wondered how Mac was doing and whether she had the same needy women responding to her with their boring thoughts on long walks and love that knew no bounds.

She paused at an unexpected subject line, the first to capture her attention: AM I HOT ENOUGH TO TIE UP? Wasting no time, she clicked on the message and devoured the contents.

Dear Skin Deep,
   Do I have your attention? I found your profile very refreshing. Certainly saves a gal a lot of time when she knows up front exactly what she's getting. I'll be candid as well. Once you see my photo, I think you're going to want to meet me. We can go out or stay in. I promise you the only strings attached will be made of satin. I look forward to our date.
   Malibu

Jordan found Malibu's photo and burst into a wide grin at the sight of a gorgeous sun-kissed blonde. Well, well. After a week of disappointment, she hadn't expected to get this lucky. Malibu was a looker all right, assuming she'd posted a photo of herself and not some model from a back issue of *In Style*. A tiny icon at the bottom of the screen signaled she was online, so Jordan began typing a reply. A little electronic foreplay could be fun.

Malibu,
   Satin? I kind of had you figured for a leather girl and I'm usually right about these matters. How about you let me dress you? I have impeccable taste and a strong desire to please.
   SD

While she waited for an answer, she glanced through the rest of her in-box and clicked open a note from Mac, inviting her to a birthday party for one of the Lewis kids. She replied quickly, accepting. She loved being part of the Lewises' extended family and had known Jeremy since he was born. As she hit Send, Malibu's response arrived.

I'll defer to your choice when it comes to accessorizing, but I was hoping your strong desire to please would involve undressing me. Well, dressed or not, I'm sure you'll be pleased with the package. Let me know if you want to get together for some unwrapping. Signing off to get my beauty rest.

Jordan was about to close her browser when a pop-up window announced that Mac was online. She clicked to initiate a live chat, typed a quick greeting, then keyed, Check out this one. Her name's Malibu. The profile says "When the sun sets, I like to let my hair down. You can run your hands through it while we paint the town." Not only does she rhyme, she looks like she would paint the town in exactly the shades I like. She's a personal trainer. What do you think?

The quick response was: Nothing personal, but I think you need some training. She's hot, at least in her picture anyway, but are looks *really* all you care about?

Give me a break. Jordan typed fast. I care about a lot of things. But, like I said last week, I'm not looking for love like you are. I don't need that. All I want is to have a good time while I am in my prime. And having a good time means getting laid without the complication of a relationship.

Maybe it's the way you look at relationships, Mac replied. If you had a better attitude, you might enjoy being in one. As long as your first love is your career, every other relationship will seem like a drain.

You're one to talk. It's not like you've had a relationship

with anyone but the Lakeside in years. That place will always come first, no matter how many lovesick "I want to snuggle up with you by a cozy fireplace" babes you meet online. Don't get me wrong, I think that's fine. Be your own partner, that's my philosophy.

Mac's response popped up as the intercom buzzed. Let's see what that gets you.

Wait, Jordan typed. She buzzed the delivery person up. It's been nice chatting with you, pal, but dinner has arrived and I'm famished.

Let me guess, Thai?

How well you know me. It looked odd, Jordan thought, seeing their online names, Skin Deep and Laker Gal, on the screen. Somehow Mac felt less familiar to her.

Jeremy's party. Let's go together, Mac offered. I'll pick you up.

It's a date, Jordan replied. She was about to type something cute about getting lucky with Malibu in the meantime, but Mac had already gone.

CHAPTER FIVE

"Ithink I'll ask Malibu if she's free for dinner Saturday night." Jordan panted a little as she pedaled up the steep hill.

"But you barely know her. In fact, I bet you haven't exchanged more than two or three e-mails." Mac's words were punctuated by heavy breathing as she fought the resistance of the sharp incline.

After spending all of Monday doing absolutely nothing, her body was reveling in this morning's exercise. She made a point of getting in several distance rides each week, often with Jordan if she wasn't working, and today was a beautiful day for biking. They'd looped around the lake and then branched off onto a trail providing a circuitous route to North Dallas. By the time they returned to their starting point, they would have traveled over thirty miles. It never ceased to amaze Mac that these bike trails took them all the way across the big city without any sense of the bustling traffic and commerce prevalent on the car-traveled streets.

"We don't need to keep e-mailing to get to know each other," Jordan said. "I know enough to know I want to meet her and see if she's everything she says she is. Hey, my seat's feeling a little wobbly. Let's pull up."

They maneuvered their bikes off the trail near a group

of picnic tables. While Jordan fiddled with her seat post, Mac grabbed a Clif Bar from her pack and broke it in half. "I understand where you're coming from," she said, handing a piece to Jordan. "But these women could be crazy for all I know. I'm not sure I want to risk a face-to-face meeting until I know someone quite well."

Jordan inspected the underside of her seat. "Suit yourself. But people can say anything online. I don't see how a blind date is any different. You've met plenty of strangers that way."

"Not to defend the blind date, because there isn't a defense for that convention, but at least on a blind date someone I know has vouched for the person. Even if they weren't entirely honest about things like looks and compatibility, at least they've taken my safety into account."

"You worry too much," Jordan said. "Life's too short. Take a risk. Make a date. If you don't, they'll think you're not serious."

"Maybe you're right."

Jordan gave her seat another once-over and announced, "Looks like I'm all fixed up. Ready?"

Mac nodded and hopped on her bike, pedaling forward slowly until she was fully clipped in. Looking over her shoulder, she called out "Race you to the park," and then pedaled away, full tilt, while Jordan was still packing her bike wrench in her seat bag.

"You beast!" Jordan yelled, clumsily trying to clip in, speed up, and simultaneously avoid a pair of Rollerbladers winding their way down the trail. She double-timed to catch up and when she did, her heavy breathing punctuated the continued conversation. "If you're concerned about safety, meet her in a busy place. Valet your car and you'll avoid the awkward 'I'll walk you to your car in the dark, deserted parking lot' moment.

For that matter, make plans to meet in the middle of the day. There's safety in sunlight."

"I guess I could do that." Mac didn't see herself gazing longingly into the eyes of the future Mrs. Lewis over lunch, however. "Dinner is much more romantic."

"Silly girl, if you believe in all that love-at-first-sight crap, then you have to believe that it can happen anytime, anywhere, don't you?"

"Been secretly reading romance novels, Dr. Love?"

"Even *I* can't avoid the constant influx of romantic imagery permeating our society," Jordan replied. "It takes all my energy to steer clear of Cupid's arrows."

"Maybe you should conserve that energy for something more productive, like—"

"Don't say it," Jordan warned. "Don't you even say it."

"What? I was going to say cycling." Mac laughed. "Use some of the energy and race me to Starbucks."

Jordan sped off, shouting, "Last one there buys!"

After a short sprint to the coffee shop, they declared a tie and clipped out of their bikes, leaving them propped them against the glass storefront. An icy blast of refrigerated air swept over their heated, sweaty bodies as they stepped indoors.

"Great day for a ride," remarked the clerk.

Jordan met a pair of deep blue eyes. They belonged to a slim, dark-haired, androgynous girl. Cute, but young. Jordan thought, *Stop staring, she's a child.* Shaking her head, she said, "Sure is. Too bad you're stuck in here."

"Yeah, I'd love to be out enjoying the day, like you and your girlfriend."

Jordan's head snapped up. Did this kid call Mac her girlfriend? She stared hard, but the girl's expression didn't reveal any hidden meaning.

Mac threw an arm over Jordan's shoulder. "I'll have my usual. I'm going to have a seat outside with the bikes."

As Mac walked away, Jordan withdrew her Starbucks card, but when the clerk reached for it, Jordan held her end of the card tight and pulled the pretty young woman toward her. "I don't do girlfriends," she whispered in her ear.

"Is that right?"

"It most certainly is. I do, however, like to have fun." Jordan released the card.

The clerk straightened. "Well, then we have something in common."

"How about you write your number on that receipt?" Jordan asked. "I'll give you a call and we can discuss our newfound common interests."

Her eyes never leaving Jordan's, the clerk scrawled something on the little white scrap of paper and pushed it toward her. "Don't worry," she whispered. "I won't tell your girlfriend."

Jordan stiffened slightly but offered a vague smile, picked up the frosty drinks, and walked outside to join Mac at one of the tables.

"What the hell took you so long?" Mac stared down into her drink. "The whipped cream is melting."

"Apparently, so is my technique. Miss Young Thing in there thinks you and I are some old married couple."

"Well, that certainly is insulting." Mac laughed. "Don't worry, Granny. I still think you're foxy, for an old lady." She curled her lips around her teeth and mimicked a toothless smile. "Do you want me to go set her straight?"

"No, dear, I don't want her to be straight. I was trying to get a date with her."

"That's great. Ditch me for a pretty young thing when

I'm reaching my prime. I should've known it would come to this."

Jordan kidded back, "Seriously, you've known me forever. What makes you think I'd make a good mate?"

Mac paused for a minute and decided to end the levity. "I think you'd make someone a great partner when you decide to quit living like a playgirl. In fact, I'm not insulted that the little girl in there thinks I have what it takes to snatch a smart, successful, beautiful woman like you off the market."

Jordan smiled and reached across the table to wipe a spot of whipped cream from Mac's upper lip. "Well, married or not, I'll always be around to keep you from having food hanging off your face."

"What a relief." Mac glimpsed something in Jordan's face that seemed at odds with her casual banter. She considered asking her friend if she'd had contact with her father lately, but decided now was not the time to broach the subject.

The subject of Dr. Jacob Wagner, a prominent Dallas plastic surgeon, was a sore spot. Jordan hadn't always been the devil-may-care, successful woman who sat across from her now. She'd taken the loss of her mother very hard and was angry with her father for choosing to be the kind of physician who focused on making people look good rather than the kind who cured disease. Even after making the same professional choice herself, she didn't seem able to reach out to him, and they still hadn't repaired the damage to their relationship.

Observing from the outside, Mac found the similarities between father and daughter completely obvious. They'd both chosen work that allowed them to experience constant success, rather than other forms of medicine, such as oncology, where successes were measured in the smallest of accomplishments. They'd both been grief-stricken at the loss of someone vital to their lives and had closed their emotions off, turning away from each other. Mac thought the rift between them was tragic, but she tiptoed around the subject because Jordan never wanted to discuss it.

She glanced at her friend. Jordan seemed lost in thought, her expression faraway. Ignoring the quick change in her mood, Mac sucked down the last of her frozen salvation and stood up. "Ready?"

"Sure." Jordan rose immediately and picked up their trash. Dropping it in the bin, she said, "I suppose I must seem like an 'older woman' to her."

"You're not still thinking about that, are you?" Mac marveled.

"You're right. I shouldn't let it get under my skin." Jordan sounded irritated. "Let's go."

They exchanged a few words about which route to take back around the lake, then walked their bikes back to the trail in silence. Parts of the trail were in disrepair, neglected in the city's priorities. To avoid a bumpy ride, they took a road that wound around part of the lake's circumference. Even light car traffic made the road more dangerous than the designated trail, but the trade-off for a smooth ride was worthwhile, especially at the end of a long ride when comfort was at a premium.

The last few miles, Mac thought about the clerk's assumption. She felt stung by Jordan's reaction. Why was she so appalled that they'd been mistaken for a couple? Mac could easily see how someone could make that assumption; they were such close friends, their bond was obvious. Still, she felt a little insulted that Jordan was so dismissive. *I'm not a bad catch,* she thought. Actually, she was great girlfriend material. She wasn't bad-looking. She owned a successful business. *And* she was available.

In fact, Jordan could do a lot worse.

❖

Shannon reached across the candlelit table and grasped her lover's hand. Looking deep into Dylan's eyes, she confessed, "It may sound crazy, but I knew I was in love with you at first glance. You stirred feelings deep inside, feelings I thought I was no longer capable of having."

A knock at the door tore Mac from the pages of *Lost Lives, Lost Loves,* and Sally Gannon poked her head in. "They're all here, Mac. If you're in the middle of something, I can start without you."

"No, I'm ready. I'll meet you at the bar in a few minutes."

The Lakeside always employed additional wait staff during the busy summer months, and with school out for summer, lots of college kids were looking for a way to earn some extra bucks. Mac conducted the hire interviews with Sally, preferring to be personally involved in every employment decision in the business. The hardest part was finding folks who were willing to work hard even though the situation wasn't permanent. The best shifts always went to the wait staff with the most tenure, meaning the summer add-ons had to work extra shifts to earn equivalent dollars. The trick was to separate the kids who were getting a summer job for the sole reason that their parents didn't want them lying around the house from those who truly needed the money. The latter motivation made for the best employees.

Mac marked her place and set the novel aside. As she stood up, she gave her calf muscles a quick rub. She was noticeably stiff from yesterday's long ride around the lake, a fact that bothered her. When she was in her twenties, recovery time was nothing, but that had changed recently, reminding her that she was turning thirty-six in a few months. It was silly to feel anxious about a birthday, but the number was starting to weigh on her. She felt as though she was in a holding pattern, waiting for the next phase of her life to begin. So far, she'd accomplished all the goals she'd set for herself. Education. Career satisfaction. Financial security. Somehow, she'd expected her other main aim in life, true love, would happen while these routine priorities consumed her time and energy.

A sense of panic gripped her as she let her gaze roam the bookshelves. She'd spent the past fifteen years reading about romance instead of living it. She'd assumed Ms. Right would walk into her world and sweep her off her feet. It seemed so simple. But where was she? What if another fifteen years passed with no sign of her? Mac didn't want to "settle" because she was afraid of being alone. She knew people who'd done that and she'd never understood their choice until now. But a strange desperation was creeping up on her. She worried that she could make a terrible mistake, that the woman of her dreams would cross her path and she would be so busy working and reading romances that she wouldn't notice her until it was too late.

As she closed her office door, she promised herself that from now on she would take the search for love much more seriously. She would stop ruling out possibilities and making excuses not to meet women. Her future wife was out there somewhere and Mac intended to find her.

"What exactly do you do?" asked gorgeous date number one, Rebeca Blixen, personal trainer at Images, the newest athletic club in Oak Lawn. Thus far their conversation had been confined to the usual "what are your favorite Dallas hot spots?" and "what do you like to do for a good time?" standards.

"Plastic surgery." Jordan paused, ready for the reaction this announcement usually inspired.

Rebeca walked right into it. "Oh, do you work for a surgeon?"

"You could say that, as I'm self-employed."

This response hung in the air for a moment and Jordan enjoyed every second as she watched realization dawn.

Rebeca's puzzled frown settled into a grin matching her own. "So, how does it feel to be your own boss?"

Pleased the discussion didn't immediately turn to one thousand and one predictable questions about life as a plastic surgeon, Jordan decided a little substantive conversation with this attractive woman wouldn't kill her. As they exchanged the basics about each other over plates of sushi, she found herself actually enjoying Rebeca's company. She'd been pleased to learn that Rebeca lived in one of the newer loft buildings downtown. Her proximity made the whole date-planning thing go much more smoothly. Jordan had picked her up in front of her building and driven them three blocks to a favorite Tex-Asian fusion restaurant in the historic Dallas Power & Light Building. Fuse served excellent cocktails on a rooftop patio with padded bamboo loungers, candlelight, fountains, and even a Jacuzzi for truly adventurous patrons. It was the perfect atmosphere for the opening scene of what Jordan had planned to be a very sensuous evening, provided her date was all she appeared to be.

As she appraised her companion one more time, she wondered why anyone bothered with an online dating service. She could easily pick up the women she wanted at the local haunts with a lot less effort, and at least then she would get to appraise their potential before committing to a full evening. Rebeca aka Malibu was a looker, that was for sure, but she could have been a dog. Athletic build with nicely proportioned female curves, shoulder-length blond hair, sea green eyes looking for nothing more than fun times with attractive women—tempting bait in a trap set for online date-seekers. But if none of the posted promises had turned out to be true, Jordan would be stuck here waiting for an opportune moment to cut their evening short. Fortunately Rebeca had been telling the truth.

Despite her luck up to this point, Jordan couldn't help but think that she should have proposed an alternative when Aimee had suggested this online nonsense. She had nothing to prove, so she didn't need to jump in as if she were a teenager unable to resist a dare. This solitary electronic pursuit of the perfect mate required a lot of up-front communication followed by dates that involved actual planning. It would have been easier, and certainly more fun, to roam the local hot spots with Mac. They were looking for different things in the women they pursued, but that didn't mean they couldn't look together, in person. Besides, Mac could probably use some quick, mindless connections to give her love life a jump start during the more complicated pursuit of a soul mate. She should make Mac join her at Sue Ellen's, her favorite Oak Lawn bar, for a night of dancing and cruising.

Picturing Mac surrounded by attractive women, all vying for her attention, Jordan suddenly felt agitated. Was she jealous? After all, she was used to being the center of attention. Surely she wouldn't begrudge her best friend the spotlight.

"Are we having dessert here, or at my place?"

Jordan nearly jumped out of her chair at the silky voice of the woman seated across from her. She stared down at the table and realized their plates had been cleared and she was too preoccupied to notice.

Rebeca's hand landed on hers. "Did I startle you?"

"Only a little." Jordan covered hastily for her inattention. "I confess. You caught me planning my next move."

"I'd like to see some of your moves. Should we go back to my place?"

"I'm ready if you are." Jordan let a slow smile slide across her face and signaled for the waiter for the check.

A few minutes later, as they waited for the valet to bring Jordan's BMW M5 around, Jordan jumped again when Rebeca's hand crept across her back and come to rest lightly at the side of her breast. "You're one jumpy gal tonight." Rebeca held her even closer, teasing, "Or are you this skittish all the time?"

Jordan recovered quickly. "Must be a little sensitive this evening. That's not a bad thing, is it?"

"Not for what I have in mind." Rebeca winked at the valet, who held open the passenger door while appearing indifferent to every word of this suggestive exchange.

As they drove to Rebeca's place, Jordan felt a familiar flutter of anticipation. She enjoyed these moments, the build-up of lust before the thrill of touch. She was as sure as she could be, after three glasses of sake, that the sex would be good tonight and there would be no strings attached. They'd both made their positions clear in their e-mails over the past week. There were no nasty surprises in store for them. This was how it should be, she reflected as they took the elevator to an upper floor of Rebeca's building, a convenient, satisfying encounter between two adults. What more could she hope for?

Rebeca's loft was as sleek as its owner. Leather, granite, steel, and hardwoods combined for a striking, modern style with clean lines. At Rebeca's direction, Jordan settled into a black leather couch in the living room while her hostess opened the liquor cabinet.

"Martini?"

"Sounds great," Jordan replied.

As Rebeca shook the cocktails, Jordan gave her another thorough checking over. Tall and toned, she looked devastating in a black silk tunic, matching pants, and high-heeled sling-back sandals.

"Tell me why a gorgeous plastic surgeon signed up with an online dating service?" Rebeca asked as she approached.

"Truth?" Jordan took the chilled martini glass she was offered. "A group of us convinced my best friend to sign up. It was sort of an intervention since she's married to her work. We figured going online would help her meet someone. She needed some coaxing, so I agreed to join in. I thought I could show her how easy it is to meet hot women without ever having to leave the office."

"What's your friend's online handle?" Rebeca asked in a conversational tone.

"Laker Gal. Her real name is Mackenzie Lewis. She owns a restaurant, the Lakeside at the south end of White Rock."

"I love the Lakeside." Rebeca's interest seemed more genuine. "Though I've never met the owner. Laker Gal...I wonder if I've seen her pic online."

"Oh, I think you'd remember. She's a beauty."

"Well, in case I don't run across her myself, be sure to thank her for me." Rebeca's voice was a purr.

Jordan nodded absently and slipped Rebeca's glass from her hand. After setting it on the end table with her own, Jordan leaned back, stretching her arm along the back of the couch. Clearly no stranger to the customary signals, Rebeca tucked herself under Jordan's arm, head tilted back, eyes slightly closed, and lips pouting for a kiss. Tingling with desire, Jordan delivered the sought-after kiss with soft deliberation, trailing her lips up Rebeca's neck as she ran her fingers through her honey-gold mane. Encouraged by a soft moan, she slid her free hand beneath the silky tunic. The feeling of soft skin enhanced by the supple silk drew a soft gasp of pleasure from her. This was definitely her idea of a good date.

She eased them both off the couch and grasped Rebeca's hand. As if she had been there many nights before, she led Rebeca through the loft to the Japanese-style platform bed at one end. Silk fell in a heap on the floor and Jordan surveyed Rebeca's figure with open appreciation. "You *are* a beauty."

"Why, thank you, Dr. Wagner. Coming from someone with your specialty, that's quite a compliment."

"Please," Jordan protested, "I'm not at work. I don't have a grease pen with me and I won't be performing any diagnostic interviews this evening."

"You've mistaken my level of self-esteem," Rebeca said. "I'm proud of how I look. This body is the result of good habits and hard work at the gym. My self-indulgences are limited to activities like the ones we are about to engage in."

"And what activities are those?" Jordan whispered in Rebeca's ear as she eased her onto the bed covers.

Reaching for the buttons on the fly of Jordan's jeans, Rebeca proceeded to demonstrate. "You know my favorite thing about these Lucky Brand jeans? The message I get when I shimmy someone out of them. Right here, inside the fly, it says 'Lucky You.' Now, who do you think will be the lucky one tonight?"

Jordan watched the downtown lights dance shadows across the gorgeous woman lying before her. A wave of pleasure washed between her thighs as Rebeca's fingers traced the message inside her fly, then found their way to the source of her discomfort. Locking lips with the seductive blonde,

Jordan kicked off her boots and stepped out of her jeans. The Luckys fell into a heap with the discarded silk.

Rebeca grasped the collar of Jordan's western-style shirt and yanked down, pulling apart the pearl snaps in one smooth motion. Finding full, naked breasts beneath, she smiled and said, "Enough looking. Get your butt on this bed and let's have some fun."

With that proclamation, she urged Jordan down on top of her and eased one of Jordan's swollen nipples into the warm and ready moisture of her mouth. The sensation sent shock waves through them both, and Jordan paused for just a moment to gaze into Rebeca's eyes. The hot invitation she saw there was as familiar as it was thrilling. She was desired, and she had the power to give this woman exactly what she wanted. All night long.

CHAPTER SIX

Mac stared at her laptop screen and gave up an exasperated sigh. Did she want to meet NoNonsense aka Charla in person this soon? What kind of message would it send? They hadn't corresponded long enough to get to anything truly personal, and their e-mail exchanges were somewhat stilted. Yet they were fairly interesting. They both liked books and reading. Charla seemed interested in the operations of the restaurant, pointing out that it was very different from her occupation as a telecommunications engineer, whatever the hell that was. Her picture looked okay. She was no beauty queen, but she seemed well groomed and didn't have any obviously scary physical attributes. Why not give it a go?

Charla,
    Would you like to meet for coffee tomorrow morning? Do you know Half Price Books on Northwest Highway? They have a wonderful coffee shop inside. How about we meet there at 10:30 a.m. Sunday?
    Looking forward to getting to know you better,
    Mackenzie

Mac conducted a quick review to make sure no egregious spelling or grammar errors marred her message and then hit

Send. Sunday morning coffee. The invitation was casual, the location low risk. She closed her laptop, refusing to watch her e-mail account like it was a pot of boiling water.

After a light dinner of creamy avocado summer soup accompanied by a garlic cheese scone, she finally checked her messages. Charla had replied an hour earlier. Her note was brief but positive. She would be there.

Well, that settled it, Mac thought. Now she had to decide what to wear. Instinctively, she picked up the phone and dialed Jordan's home phone number. After receiving no answer, she tried her cell. As the phone rang, she remembered that Jordan had planned to ask Malibu out for a *second* date tonight. Disappointed, she hung up before the switch to voicemail. She had wanted to tell Jordan that she wasn't a chicken after all and had taken a chance on an online prospect. Not that Jordan cared. She was off hunting on her own.

Mac felt an unidentifiable twinge, but instantly set her unease aside. She could pick out her own clothes; she didn't need Jordan for everything. Resigned to making a wardrobe choice without her best friend's advice, she visualized the potential selections in her mind's eye. Later that night, as she got ready for bed, she laid out a pair of jeans, blue suede shoes, and a short-sleeved light blue hoodie. Casual, but hip, she concluded. Totally appropriate for a coffee date.

She rewarded herself with some suitable bedtime reading.

Dylan's glance swept down ducking her paramour's rapt gaze. She fought the urge to echo the words, resisting the easy, but unsure path. Sensing the gathering uncertainty from the woman waiting silently within her reach, she gathered words to fill the void. "Darling, I love being with you. I feel amazing in your presence."

She watched and knew Shannon caught the subtlety of her dodged response. Tears formed as Dylan felt the force of feeling that was growing between them. Sobs choked her next words, but she knew she needed to share everything with her new lover. "I have something to confess."

Mac paused, once more bothered that she hadn't been able to reach Jordan. It was unreasonable to expect her to be on call for fashion consultations, and Mac was used to leaving messages. They were both busy women, and she respected Jordan's space. But she'd never felt the way she did now, that she had something to prove to Jordan. She closed *Lost Lives* and rolled onto her side. Jordan's comments at Starbucks the previous weekend still rankled and Mac felt a growing need to prove something to her. Jordan might not see her as partner material but someone else would, and when that happened Mac was going to enjoy flaunting her new love.

Blinded by the sharp sunlight glancing off the hood of her car, Jordan hurriedly reached for her Fendi shades and unlocked the door of her M5. She slid into the driver's seat, enjoying the way the cushioned leather fit against her body. The crisp fall air fueled her appetite as she drove with the top down through Oak Lawn to her favorite weekend brunch spot, La Duni. Lots of midnight exercise motivated her to select a dozen of her favorite pastries. She sipped on a rich mocha at the bar while waiting for the staff to box her Latin treats: guava and cheese glorias, orange brioche, mantecadas, and pecan maple pastry, complete with lemon curd and raspberry butter. This gayborhood spot made for some excellent people-watching, and she reluctantly pulled herself away when the hostess brought her check.

The crowd was growing thick at the popular bakery and Jordan had to wait several minutes for the valet to bring her car around. While she waited, she tried Mac's number again, a little guilty that she was only replying to last night's missed calls twelve hours later. But Mac took most Sundays off and could be counted on to share this box of goodies over a pot of coffee while Jordan regaled her with the highlights of her two dates with Rebeca. After the fifth ring, Mac's voicemail announced that she couldn't get to the phone right now and invited the caller to leave a message. Jordan clicked off and decided on Plan B. Mac was probably in the shower and would be out by the time Jordan arrived.

The drive across town was short on a Sunday morning, as most Dallas cars were either nestled in garages or parked at churches and favorite brunch spots. Jordan pulled into Mac's long driveway, admiring her friend's restored 1920s bungalow. The house was vastly different from Jordan's high-rise loft, which said a lot about their personalities. Mac had grown up in a warm family environment and seemed to replicate that past in each part of her life without even realizing it. The Lakeside was casual and welcoming, and Mac's home was the kind of place that seemed to cry out for Thanksgiving dinners and a dog in the yard. Jordan had fond memories of walking in the door and being greeted with hugs by Mac's parents.

The Lewises fit together seamlessly. As an outsider, Jordan could see they had their issues. Running their business together caused a lot of tension, but they worked through their problems and tried to keep their family from noticing that they had any. She remembered hearing whispered fights sometimes, over whether the diner was consuming their lives and keeping them from other dreams. They could never seem to get away and they worried about finances and having enough to help all their kids in school. Yet they were glass-half-full kinds of people. They stayed together in the face of conflict, their pact as a couple too strong to be defeated by external challenges.

Jordan couldn't imagine having a relationship like that. She thought about Rebeca and laughed. None of the women she dated would ever consider settling for a life like that. The thought made her stop a moment as she parked behind a truck in the driveway. Would it be "settling" to know she could depend completely on another person, no matter what? Jordan shrugged off the thought. Ties like that were for people who wanted children. She had different priorities. And besides, she didn't have to be in a long-term relationship to have someone who truly cared about her. She could count on Mac.

Jordan lingered as she got out of her vehicle and breathed in the earthly aroma. Spying rakes, shovels, and leaf blowers poking out from the iron grate lining the truck bed, she assumed that Mr. Diaz was somewhere on the property. The crisp scent of freshly cut grass hung in the air, confirming her suspicions. She spotted the gardener and called, "Hey, Mr. Diaz. Is Mackenzie home?"

He propped his rake against a garden cart. "She went to the bookstore."

"Well, that wasn't very nice of her," Jordan joked. "I brought breakfast and gossip. How dare she get started this early on a Sunday morning."

"She left about ten minutes ago," Mr. Diaz said, dragging a bag of lawn clippings toward her. "I wanted to talk to her about changing the flower beds, but she said she was running late."

Jordan scratched her head at the report. What in the world could Mac have been late for at the bookstore? "Well, why don't you take this box of goodies, then?"

She thrust the La Duni box into his hands and returned to her car. With the engine idling, she vacillated for a few seconds, reluctant to bust in on Mac if she was trying to take some time out on her own. But she and Mac often spent hours at Half Price Books, and their tastes were very different, so they usually split up to browse the aisles, then met back in the coffee shop to share the spoils of their hunt.

Jordan sped uptown hoping to catch her. Apparently lots of folks had decided to do their Sunday morning at the bookstore. She had to circle the parking lot for at least ten minutes, vying for a space. Finally, her parking karma kicked in and she grabbed a spot near the coffee shop entrance of the store. She glanced at herself in the rearview mirror, brushed a few windblown hairs back into place, and slid out of the car. Her shades barely provided enough protection from the sun reflecting from the large plate glass windows along the entire front of the store. Using one hand as a shield, she used the other to open the door to the coffee shop and walked into the icy cold refrigerated air all Texas businesses used to combat the searing summer heat.

It took a moment for her eyes to adjust to the indoor lighting. Almost immediately, she spotted Mac across the room, enjoying a cup of java. Smiling, she started to wave but stopped before her hand could reach the air. Who in the world was that woman sitting with Mac? It wasn't any of their friends. Whoever she was, she was certainly acting very friendly, leaning in close and hanging on Mac's every word. She was fairly nice looking but rather plain, with mousy brown hair combed in a nondescript style, average build, and forgettable features. Her ensemble was a boring combination of black slacks, a taupe silk blouse, and low-heeled black leather pumps. She looked a little dressy for the bookstore. In fact, this mystery woman looked like she was on a date.

A date? Jordan backed up a step. Was this what the Internet had dredged up? This woman wasn't Mac's type, was she? Someone as gorgeous as Mac would certainly want to date a woman whose good looks matched her own and who didn't dress up to go to the bookstore, for crying out loud. Jordan's thoughts jolted her again as she realized, despite her obsession with beautiful things, that she rarely spent time thinking about her best friend's beauty. She'd always taken for granted that Mac was good-looking, with her sassy blond hair, big brown eyes, and that trim, athletic body. She could have anyone she wanted. The very thought made Jordan feel a little agitated.

"Jordan? What are you doing here?"

Jordan nearly jumped out of her skin as she realized she'd been staring at Mac and the overdressed woman for who knew how long. She plastered a smile on her face and strode toward their table. "Oh, hi, Mac. I was on my way home and decided to swing by and pick up a copy of the *Voice*." She casually referenced the local LGBT newspaper.

"Kind of out of your way, isn't it?"

"Well, you don't know where I've been now, do you?" Jordan smirked and offered a hand to the mousy woman. "I don't believe we've met."

"We haven't. My name is Charla." A limp handshake followed.

"Nice to meet you, Charla." Jordan did her best to sound warm and friendly instead of horrified by Mac's decision to meet this unimpressive woman. "Come here often?"

"Actually, it's my first time. It's quaint here. I love books, but I usually shop at Barnes and Noble down the street. This store is very…eclectic." Charla's tone gave the impression "eclectic" was a polite term reserved for things she didn't like.

Jordan had to speak in defense of her favorite bookstore.

"Well, this store certainly does have a lot of character. There's no telling what you'll find on a given day."

"True. However, most of the time I know exactly what I am shopping for and I like the convenience of knowing it will be in stock. I don't like to have to rely on my ability to stumble across rejections from someone else's personal library."

Jordan turned toward Mac, making little effort to hide her grimace. "Is this a date or what?"

Mac's face, already red from watching the tense exchange, deepened in color. "Yep. We were getting to know each other. Thanks for stopping by to say hello."

Jordan stared at her in disbelief. She recognized the tone, but was taken aback that Mac had blatantly dismissed her. "Yeah, well, I'll see you around." She waved at the nonentity. "It was nice to meet you, Charo."

Watching Jordan's retreating back, Mac refrained from correcting the name. "Sorry," she mumbled, knowing she could expect a phone call later and a lot of grief about this encounter.

"Is she one of your exes?" Charla asked.

A sharp ringing rousted Jordan from a deep afternoon sleep. She struggled to keep the phone cradled against her shoulder as she sat up in bed. "Who is this?"

"You know who this is. What are you doing asleep in the middle of the day?"

"Oh, Mac, it's you." Jordan yawned. "Slow down with the questions, will you? I was taking a little nap. I didn't get a lot of rest last night."

"That's no excuse being an ass to my date this morning," Mac growled.

"Give me a break. I wasn't being an ass. I was merely

expressing my opinion. Besides, it's not like you're going to see her again." Sleep deprivation didn't keep Jordan from counting the beats of silence that followed. "You're not, are you? Going to see her again?"

"What if I am?"

"Oh, honey, she's not your type. She's not anyone's type. She's the kind of boring, buttoned-up, frumpy woman who has to resort to finding someone online because, in person, she sends cool chicks like us running. She's what you get when you post a sappy profile like yours."

"I'm going to try to ignore the fact that you've just insulted me. For all you know, Charla may be exactly the kind of woman I'm looking for."

"If Charla's your type, then I don't know you very well." Jordan could feel her voice rising and decided to take a different tack. "Come on, Mac. What about all the dynamic leading ladies in those romances you devour? Charla wouldn't even rate a bit part."

"That's fiction. I'm looking for a real life partner, not a paperback love affair."

"You create your own reality, Mac. Women like that are only fictional if you refuse to let the possibility become reality. I went out with someone I met online last night and she was hot. Hell, we even had good conversation during dinner."

"Jordan, I *am* being realistic. Someday you're going to stop living in the fast lane and realize life isn't about how many hot women you can bed. I want to find someone to share my life, not for a night, but for a lifetime. So I'm looking at more qualities than looks and sexual prowess. Is that so hard for you to understand?"

Stung, Jordan retorted, "Well, I can guarantee that if you don't see an attractive face looking back at you after a night of clumsy sex, then a lifetime is going to seem very long indeed."

"Not as long as spending it alone," Mac replied. "I don't even know why we bother having these conversations. You're never going to change."

"You're damn right about that. I will always want the best and never settle for less. I never figured you for the settling kind."

After a few long seconds of silence, Mac asked, "Jordan, are you jealous?"

Jordan almost dropped the phone. Jealous? Could it be that she was jealous? Of what? She loved Mac dearly, but she wasn't attracted to her that way. Was she?

"Did you hang up on me?" Mac's voice jolted her from her disturbing train of thought.

"No, I'm still here."

"Well?"

"I don't know what you mean. Why would I be jealous?"

"You tell me."

"Don't play games with me, Mac. I just woke up and I'm feeling kind of cranky."

"What I'm saying is that you always seem to have a hand in helping me pick out my dates, but Charla's someone I picked out all on my own, with no input from you. Do you think maybe you're a tiny bit jealous that I can pick my own dates?"

Ah, Jordan thought, *she doesn't think I am attracted to her, she just thinks I am a control freak.* Embarrassed that she'd jumped to the wrong conclusion, she replied, "Well, I don't know what I would be jealous of. You don't seem to be doing such a great job all on your own."

She wasn't sure if Mac even heard the last couple of words. Her reply was inaudible over the sound of the phone slamming down.

CHAPTER SEVEN

"I need you to be brutally honest," Mac said. "Why do you think I've never been lucky in love?"

"Lucky in love, huh? That's an interesting way of putting it." Aimee paused as she buttered a roll. "I don't think luck, bad or good, has anything to do with the fact that you haven't been in a long-term relationship. You're no different than Jordan in that respect."

"Hold on a minute," Mac protested.

"Hear me out. I'm saying you're married to your restaurant the same way she's married to that image of herself as a playgirl. Be brutally honest with yourself and 'fess up. How many times have you chosen this place over the arms of a woman who was trying to care about you? I can think of a few who gave up once they found they couldn't compete."

Mac took in the full force of Aimee's words. "Wow, that's pretty brutal. I guess I always thought if a woman cared about me, she would understand work comes first at times."

"Honey, there's a difference between occasional interruptions to your love life because of a crisis at work and occasional interruptions to your work to have a love life. It's never taken long for your lovers to realize *they're* the interruption."

"Again, that's brutal."

"But honest. And they must feel pretty darn low on the totem pole when they see that you're perfectly willing to interrupt work for your friends. When was the last time you told Jordan you were too busy to bike, or go to the bookstore, or whatever?"

"Easy now. That's different. Jordan and I have been friends forever. Friendships have to be cultivated and cared for."

"Same goes for love, sweetie." Aimee slid her soup bowl to one side. "Romantic relationships take time, care, and cultivation. It's not like those romance novels you swallow whole."

"I've been on a lot of dates." Mac knew she sounded defensive.

"Wrong. Double-dating with Jordan doesn't count as a date."

"Give me a break. We do all the regular date things."

"Let me guess, Jordan usually picks you up first, right? Then you pick up your dates. You go somewhere, the four of you, and most of the evening you and Jordan talk to each other until it's time to split up. She drops off your date, then you, and then takes off with her flavor of the evening. You guys hook up the next day, and you listen to tales about her night of passion. Am I close?"

"Oh, my God. I'm the lamest person there is."

"You're not lame, dear. You're in a rut. A very comfortable rut. As long as you continue to buddy up with Jordan in your love life, you don't have to think for yourself, let alone commit. You don't find the dates yourself, so you aren't personally invested enough to make a go of it. Hell, you don't even drive or decide where you are going."

"For your information, I went on a date yesterday. A woman I picked entirely by myself. Jordan hadn't even met her."

"Someone you met online?"

"Yep."

"How was it? I'm thinking not great or you would be spending this afternoon pleasantly reminiscing instead of conducting an analysis of your romantic potential."

"It was horrible," Mac admitted. "Her name's Charla. She's stuffy, self-righteous, and frumpy. It was all I could do to muddle through a conversation with her. To top it off, Jordan showed up and they starting sparring."

"Slow down, girl. Jordan showed up on your date?"

"It was weird. I asked Charla to meet me at Half Price Books for coffee. I figured it was a good setting for a casual 'let's see where this goes' kind of date. We're sitting there, sipping mochas and wading through tedious conversation when I look up and see Jordan across the room staring at us. It was truly strange. To top it off, I was overcome by this weird need to make Jordan think Charla was a splendid date and we wanted to be left alone, so I totally brushed her off."

"Who, Charla?"

"No, Jordan. I brushed her off, but she wouldn't leave. She stayed and started asking Charla questions. I practically had to tell her to get out."

"How embarrassing."

"Yeah. Jordan was the one pushing me to make a date with whoever I met online. I took her advice and it's almost like she was mad about it."

"Interesting."

"What do you mean?"

"Well, I think it's interesting that Miss I'll Date Anyone Hot Who Looks My Way thinks your dates need to be screened, and she's the person to do it."

"Jordan's always been protective about who I date. Come to think of it, no one has ever measured up to her standards."

Mac sighed. "I shouldn't give her a hard time. I'm sure she means well."

"Are you?" When Mac didn't answer, Aimee said, "I have some advice. You aren't going to like it. Find your own love life, on your own. Do your own searches, chat with someone you pick out entirely on your own, and make a date. Decide if you enjoyed the date before you ever compare notes with anyone else about it. And that means Jordan, in particular."

"Damn, that's harsh. What are friends for if I can't ask for advice?"

"Your friends will support your decisions and trust your judgment. If they don't, then what kind of friends are they?"

"Are you saying Jordan isn't supportive? She's been pushing me to find someone."

"I know Jordan loves you and wants to help," Aimee said. "But I'm saying give this a chance and who knows what you might find. All by yourself."

< Malibu > You sure know how to show a girl a good time.

< Skin Deep > Right back at you. What are you doing right now?

< Malibu > Doing a little good-night surfing when I saw you online.

< Skin Deep > I see. Looking for another hot date?

< Malibu > Maybe. I found your friend the restaurateur.

< Skin Deep > I see. Well, if you want to know more about her I can dispel the mystery.

< Malibu > No, that would take all the fun out of imagining her. I love fantasizing.

< Skin Deep > Well, if you want any help with your fantasies, you know where to find me.

Rereading the chat from last night, Jordan frowned. Rebeca's curiosity about Mac was getting under her skin and she wasn't sure why. Funny she should care. It wasn't as if she expected anything more than a few good times with Rebeca. She wasn't looking for something more serious than that. The sex had been incredible on both their dates, but there was no shortage of beautiful women in this city who would be more than willing to join her for a romp. All the same, it bothered her that Rebeca had joked about fantasizing over Mac. Somehow, that felt off-limits.

Jordan closed her laptop as her office manager tapped on the door. With obvious displeasure, Grace announced, "There's a Ms. Blixen here to see you. She doesn't have an appointment, but she's very persistent."

Jordan grinned at her tone. Grace Cunningham, RN, had served as Jordan's assistant, office manager, and sergeant-at-arms since the day she'd entered private practice. Grace had spent years working for Jordan's dad, Dr. Jacob Wagner, and had been indispensable to his practice. When Jordan's mother died of breast cancer, Grace became even more indispensable, helping him get a distraught Jordan through her tortured high school years by trying to fill in some of the gaps left by her extremely dynamic mother. Jordan knew she held a special place in Grace's heart and when she finished her fellowship at Presbyterian Hospital and opened her own practice, she stole Grace away from the elder Dr. Wagner without a qualm. Grace was fiercely protective, and that was one of the reasons they worked so well together. She guarded Jordan's time from distractions, allowing her to focus on her clientele.

"It's okay," Jordan said. "I know Ms. Blixen. Send her in."

A moment later, Rebeca sashayed into the room and slowly turned, taking in the large office and its furnishings. Jordan's wasn't a typical doctor's office, with diplomas, certificates, and a few anatomical models here and there. Hers was more like a luxurious living room, complete with a plush sofa and love seat, fine art, a plasma TV, and a fifty-gallon aquarium. A well-stocked granite wet bar replaced the usual sterile sink area.

"I was in your neck of the woods and thought I would stop by and see where the good doctor works," Rebeca said. "This is downright opulent. Are you sure this is your office?"

"Not your standard clinic digs, huh?" Jordan kept her tone casual, unwilling to show irritation at the unexpected visit. "One of the most important rules of sales is dress for success. Think my office makes me look like the most successful plastic surgeon in Dallas?"

"Is that important to you?"

"Well, cosmetic surgery is different from most other fields of medicine," Jordan said. "Most of my clients are people who've chosen to have surgery, not out of a life-or-death need, but out of some emotional need. They need to feel comfortable talking about those emotions and this atmosphere helps. It's not medicine-y. It's more like a plush therapist's office. Second, since most of the surgery that I perform is elective, therefore not paid for by insurance, people tend to be pretty picky when they're paying out of their own pocket. They usually want a good-looking doctor with an upscale practice." She waved at the room. "I think I convey that, don't you?"

"Complete understatement."

"What are you doing here?" Jordan asked, surprised that she wasn't happy to see her. "I thought you weren't into cosmetic surgery."

"I guess I was curious. What would you suggest if I wanted something done?"

"Why mess with nature when she's been so good to you?" Jordan shrugged. "I suppose I could squeeze you in if there something special you had in mind."

"Darling, I may need something special, but surgery won't be necessary." Rebeca slid her bottom onto Jordan's desk and crossed her long legs, revealing an expanse of firm thigh. "You know, I almost went to the wrong office. There's another J. Wagner doing plastic surgery in Dallas."

"I had no idea," was Jordan's clipped reply. Of her friends, only Mac and Aimee knew that Jacob Wagner was her father. Since Jordan barely acknowledged his existence, out of respect for her they rarely brought up the other Dr. Wagner.

"You don't know him?" Rebeca failed to sense a change in her demeanor. "It seems like you would have crossed paths since you're both in the same profession."

Jordan dodged the question. "You'd be surprised how many plastic surgeons there are in Dallas."

"Well, I am sure that's the case. It seems odd that your names are similar and you've never even heard of him."

Jordan stood and started walking around her desk. "I don't get why it matters to you. My next client will be here in a moment. Do you mind leaving this way?" She pointed to a fairly well disguised outline of a door near the wet bar. "It's a private hall. Grace's office is at the end and she'll see you out."

Ignoring the brush-off, Rebeca asked, "Are you free for lunch? I have a few errands to run in the neighborhood and I'll be close by around noon. We could eat in if you like." Her expression suggested food would not be the only item on the menu.

Jordan shook her head. "No, thanks. I keep a tight schedule on Mondays."

Rebeca seemed to detect the coolness in her mood and tried to rally her with a flirtatious smile. "Kiss to get you through the day?"

The newly formed layer of ice was not to be broken. "I think I can make it without. Thanks and have a good afternoon."

CHAPTER EIGHT

"This is such a lame way to spend a Thursday night," Mac growled into the phone. She tried to do something relaxing on Thursday nights since she usually worked long shifts on Fridays. Surfing the Internet for love didn't fit her idea of relaxing.

"Do you want me to come over?" Aimee asked. "I'm in my nightgown, settled in to watch a *Charlie's Angels* marathon, but I'll gladly throw on a pair of jeans and head your way."

"No, I don't want to tear you away from your sweethearts. I called Jordan, but she has to work late."

"Thanks, pal," Aimee griped. "You're not supposed to let a girl know she's second choice. Are you sure Jordan had to work? I think she secretly likes the online dating and has probably amassed a long list of women she's working her way through."

"I won't even dignify your speculation with a response." Mac felt that twinge again. Was she jealous of Jordan burning up the Web with her quest for new flames? "Maybe you're right," she told Aimee. "Judging by the lack of good prospects, Jordan's probably had her way with most of these babes, and now they're off swooning somewhere in the aftermath."

"Say, why are you calling me? I thought you were going to try this on your own for a while, relying on your own instincts."

"My instincts are telling me to run and hide. I called you for a pep talk, now let's have it."

"Okay, let's pick someone for you to meet. Who are the top three candidates?"

"There isn't a top three. There isn't one woman on here I am interested in having an online chat with, let alone meeting in person."

"Oh, you are a lost cause. Quit being so damn picky. Read me a profile, anyone's profile," Aimee encouraged.

"Yeah, okay. Then you'll see how hopeless this whole exercise is. Here's one, she goes by NoBonesAboutIt, which already gives me the willies on several different levels. No, wait. I just got a new e-mail. It's from FanningtheFlame. I haven't seen her profile online, but listen to this."

Mac reviewed most of the e-mail in silence, but selected a couple of the best lines to read aloud as she went along.

I've been reading your profile every day this week and today I finally got up the courage to subscribe to this site so I could write to you. I, like you, have spent my life working hard for many things, but none of the things I've acquired have made my heart beat faster than it did when I read your feelings about love and relationships. I agree that a strong relationship requires nurturing and that passion and commitment will fan the flames and keep the fire alive. I'd like to meet you and see if our first glance ignites feelings that will burn forever. I invite you to read my profile and contact me if it sparks your interest.

"Whew, it's getting hot in here," Aimee sassed. "Does she look as good as she sounds?"

"I can't think of a better word than 'hot' to describe her. Where the hell has she been hiding?"

"Honey, she's been sitting in the wings, waiting for the right moment to come out and play with you." Aimee adopted a begging tone. "Please tell me you're going to play with her."

"You're hopeless. I promise I'll write her back. And if she can keep up her end of the conversation for a couple of rounds of chat, I swear, I'll make a date with her."

"Good girl. Now, if you don't need me for anything else…"

"Go back to your Angels. Tell Kelly I said hello."

"Will do."

Mac was already rereading the e-mail from FanningtheFlame before Aimee clicked off the line. Composing her response in her head, she spoke her most pressing thought out loud, "Are you for real?"

"Where the hell is she?" Jordan muttered as she typed "Malibu" into the search directory for the third time.

She stared in disbelief at the message: NO RESULTS FOUND. That was weird. Jordan felt bad about the abrupt way she'd ushered Rebeca out of her office earlier that week. Rebeca had called several times since, but Jordan had been meeting with patients or was in surgery on each occasion. Composing an apology in her head, she'd spent a good half hour online looking for her. She reached for the cordless phone near her bed, then realized she didn't know her phone number. She'd made a point of "forgetting" to ask for it. But she knew where Rebeca lived.

Jordan contemplated making a personal appearance to convey regret for her actions. She'd been a shit this week, snapping at a woman she barely knew, for no good reason, and getting irrationally impatient with everyone she spoke to. She'd tried to contact Mac, wanting to smooth things over, but Mac had been distant all week, surely on account of Jordan's disapproval of her dating choices.

Placing the laptop on her nightstand, she slid her feet into the worn Gucci loafers resting at her bedside. She wasn't going to sit here all evening feeling helpless. It was always easier to smooth over hurt feelings face-to-face. She moved to the mirror and gave herself a quick once-over. Her slightly wrinkled pale green cotton shirt and weathered Lucky jeans would be fine for a casual late-night visit. Besides, Jordan remembered, Rebeca liked the Luckys.

Nosing the Beemer out of the parking garage adjacent to her building, Jordan noted that the traffic was light, even for a late Thursday evening. She attributed the nearly barren streets to the misty rain starting to fall. On weeknights, the Deep Ellum bars featured live local color that drew alternative music junkies from the entire metroplex, usually in droves. But inconvenient, uncovered parking meant it took only a little rain to ward off all but the die-hard fans.

Heading west on Main Street the few short blocks to Rebeca's apartment, she contemplated what she was doing. *I'm dropping in to apologize for being a jerk earlier this week. I was pretty abrupt and I know it's because Rebeca mentioned dad.* Of course, Rebeca couldn't know that the other Dr. Wagner was her father. How was Jordan going to explain her reaction without explaining what was behind it? She had no desire to get into a discussion about her father. Did she even owe Rebeca an explanation? It wasn't like they were dating. They'd gone out twice. Their conversations were little more than foreplay. She didn't know the woman. Hell, she didn't even know her phone number.

As she approached Pearl Street, her musings turned to resolution and she abruptly changed lanes, choosing right over left. Right led to Oak Lawn and all the promises of the Dallas lesbian nightlife. Hoping the rain hadn't deterred all the beautiful women from coming out, Jordan decided to start the evening fresh, no apologies, no regrets. Leaving Rebeca's building far behind, she drove directly to Sue Ellen's.

The usual suspects were all in residence. Stepping into the shadowy bar, Jordan paused to take stock of the room. The place was crowded with women jockeying for the best position to order the drink special from one of the three female bartenders. One beautiful, one foxy, one tomboyish, they rushed around each other trying to keep up with the demands of the women vying for their attention. Holding back from the crowd, Jordan enjoyed watching the dance. The choreography never changed no matter the composition of the audience.

Though she was standing a couple of rows back from the crowded bar railing, her status as a regular came with perks. After she placed her order, the bartender walked out from behind the bar to make a personal delivery. Sidling up close, she wrapped an arm around Jordan's waist and placed the longneck Miller Lite in her hand. "Haven't seen you on a school night for a while. How've you been?"

Jordan took a long draft from the bottle and appraised the woman attached to her hip. Short, spiked brown hair with sandy highlights, slim hips, tiny waist, and a perfect round ass all showed out nicely on her small frame. She wasn't Jordan's type, but her androgynous, edgy, ageless looks certainly turned heads. A group lining the front row of the bar glanced back at them, torn between enjoying the picture they cut and mourning the loss of their drink maker.

Noticing the glances, Jordan warned her hipmate, "If you don't head back soon, I fear the masses will come looking for you."

"Promise me a dance before you leave?"

"I may not be staying long."

"Well, if a beautiful woman hasn't whisked you away by the time I get my break, you're all mine."

"Deal," Jordan replied, knowing it wasn't. The banter was safe and meaningless since they both knew they would never hook up. Though the bartender would probably be a willing participant in any extracurricular activity Jordan offered, Jordan came here often and wasn't going to risk losing one of her playgrounds over a one-night stand and possible hurt feelings.

Leaving her spot near the bar, she wandered by the dance floor. Apparently Thursday nights were made for drinking, not aerobics, so there weren't too many women gyrating to the music. Jordan pushed through the patio doors and settled into one of the wire mesh chairs that lined the outdoor room. Angling her seat to give her a balanced view of the patio and the nightlife on the street, she took another deep draft of her beer. She remembered the first time she and Mac had come here, fake ID's at the ready. Seniors at East Dallas High, they'd ditched their homecoming dates, changed into club wear, and struck out to the bar they'd read about. After Jordan's mother died, her father never paid much attention to what she did, leaving her free to explore all she wanted. Somehow she and Mac, both questioning their sexuality, had been lucky enough to find each other in the sea of students at EDH. Together they'd learned about gay life on the sly, reading books and magazines that confirmed that it was okay to feel the things they felt.

Their first night at Sue Ellen's had been like a child's first trip to Disney World, full of glitzy attractions, wild rides, and tasty treats. The strong beat of the music, the flashing lights, and the few drinks they'd managed to get women to buy them animated their newfound sexual feelings. Jordan imagined familiarity was the reason they'd turned to each other. She recalled the moment Mac had leaned in and kissed her full on the mouth. The taste of her tongue was sweet but the effect was searing. At first they'd melted into an embrace, but then Jordan's initial response was replaced with fear, causing her to push Mac away. Mac, still woozy from the effect of the passionate kiss, seemed slow to realize the rejection wasn't temporary. Eyes hazy with longing looked deep into Jordan's, and she'd sensed an intensity of feeling in Mac that worried her. By contrast, her own feelings seemed too shallow. She felt almost numb.

In hindsight, she could see that her mother's death and her father's withdrawal had stuffed feelings like love deep down inside, compacted into unrecognizable forms, not likely to spring back to life. To allow them to surface was to invite pain, for her and for the people who loved her. She didn't have what it took to weather love's storms without completely shutting down. Mac came from a family where love was the way things were. Her parents were in love and loved her. Her siblings were loyal beyond measure. Seventeen-year-old Mackenzie Lewis didn't know pain, and Jordan wasn't going to drag her into the depths of hers. She'd been certain the pursuit of anything romantic would destroy the fast friendship she was desperate to keep.

Ignoring the plea in her eyes, Jordan had announced, "Now we've practiced on each other, let's try our skills on some of the babes in here."

Mac's features shuffled quickly into composure as she realized that Jordan was done with their tiny foray of passion.

In all the years they'd known each other, she'd never once alluded to that moment, and Jordan had stopped thinking about what her silence conveyed.

A voice, and the gentle press of a hand on her shoulder shook Jordan from her reflections and she glanced up expecting to see one of the cocktail waitresses. Instead she stared up into big brown eyes that locked her with their gaze.

"Would you like another beer?" the stranger asked.

Breathtaking, Jordan thought. The face that featured those baby browns also boasted fair smooth skin that would be soft to the touch. Resolving to find out just how soft, Jordan replied, "I'd rather dance, if that's an acceptable alternative."

Nodding, the beautiful stranger held out her hand and Jordan grasped it, moving them back inside to the dance floor. Joining a few other couples, they swayed to the R&B dance vibe of Rihanna's "Good Girl Gone Bad." Jordan placed her hands on the woman's hips and began a gradual ascent. A song and dance later, her hands framed her dance partner's face and she leaned in for a long, slow kiss that stretched through several verses and a chorus.

The stranger leaned back and offered, "I live close by."

Jordan's nod was the only reply, but a clear signal. The woman took her by the hand and led her out the door. Her white Mercedes convertible transported them a few blocks away to the vast circular drive that fronted one of Oak Lawn's new high-rise condo buildings. Though the hour was late, the dutiful valet snapped to attention and opened the driver's door, leaving Jordan to fend for herself. She stepped out and followed her hostess through the large glass doors held open by a man dressed in full doorman regalia. They walked in silence to a bank of elevators. Once inside and riding upward, the stranger pinned Jordan to the back wall and kissed her with steady force and purpose. Jordan's body responded without reservation. Grabbing fistfuls of the thick, platinum mane, she pulled the full sensuous lips closer.

The elevator stopped on the twenty-fifth floor, and the stranger whispered, "Should we adjourn to my apartment?"

Again, Jordan nodded assent.

Dim lights made mysterious the shadowy exchange as they tangled together inside the woman's home. Drunk on the moment, Jordan moved in a trance, following the flaxen-haired siren, oblivious to any rocky pitfalls lurking in the shadows. She saw something of herself in the easy confidence with which this woman led her to bed, firmly pushed her down, and brazenly began removing her clothes. She watched, as if in a mirror, and it was almost a game to predict the next move: *Now, she'll lean in to deliver light kisses along my neck, her thigh positioned to give a small, teasing pressure designed to drive me to distraction. In response to my begging moans, she'll bump up the pressure, her tongue playing promises in my mouth, assuring arousal that will send me over the edge.*

Despite her vantage point, Jordan's body started to feel the sensations her mind described and she wondered at her own loss of control. Was this how she made other women feel? How could they possibly survive the total loss of control? How did this beauty know she could have her like this? Out of her hazy musings, a question broke through. "How do you know what I want?"

Her words hung in the air. The nameless vixen paused in her ministrations, undaunted by the query, and answered simply, "Mind-blowing sex with no strings attached. Everyone knows that's what you want."

Declaration delivered, she bent down and nipped at Jordan's mouth, her hot tongue seeking entrance. Like a diver, having tasted the depth of her prowess but now desperately trying to cut the water's surface, Jordan kicked her way back to awareness, pulling away.

"I'm leaving," she announced, throwing her legs over the side of the bed and reaching for her shirt.

"Don't leave, Doctor. We're just getting started." Arms circled Jordan's waist, unbuttoning as fast as Jordan could fasten.

With more force than she intended, Jordan jerked the tail of her shirt from the woman's grasp, shedding several buttons in the process. Both women stared at the bits of metal as they clanked on the floor, swirled in place, and rolled off into silence. Jordan grasped her shirttail with both hands and moved quickly to the door. Moments later she emerged from the elevator, catching the knowing glance of the dolled-up doorman. Ignoring his attempts to beat her to the tall glass doors, she swiftly made her exit.

Early summer's curse was limited to sweltering days. The night air at this time in the season was still bearable and even offered a light breeze. Jordan walked the blocks back to Sue Ellen's to retrieve her car, welcoming the fresh air as it breathed her back to awareness. What was wrong with her? She'd left a beautiful woman who was ready and willing. Ruefully, she reflected that she herself had been ready and willing. Was she that easy to make? *Lesbian seeks lay: I don't care what your favorite food is, whether you like to dance fast or slow—hell, I don't even have to know your name. You must be a great fuck. No further information necessary.*

The walk back to the bar seemed to take forever as she grappled with the realization that she no longer cared for the reputation she'd tried her whole life to cultivate. As she crossed Cedar Springs, she glanced at the patio where the night's misadventure had begun. Squinting to dispel the distraction of the wrought iron railing, she saw only the memory of that night when she and Mac had been young and curious. Though cynical even then, she couldn't completely sever herself from her yearnings. Now, looking back, she recognized the force behind her cynicism. Fear. Fear of loss, fear of pain, fear of love. Funny, almost twenty years later, the fear was still there but she'd learned to call it by other, more acceptable, names: independence, control, fortitude.

Slipping behind the wheel of her M5, Jordan leaned back and felt the memory of young Mackenzie's lips meeting hers. All these years later, fear still fought the feeling away, yet something of the yearning rushed back.

CHAPTER NINE

R esisting the tease of the tiny envelope icon in the corner of her laptop screen, Mac poured herself a humongous cup of French roast and added a hefty measure of cream. Carrying the cup of java, she left the kitchen and the beckoning e-mail and strolled outdoors to retrieve the morning paper. The Friday edition featured new restaurant reviews and Mac liked to start off the weekend by assessing the competition. Pausing under the large pecan tree, she stretched her arms over her head, soaking up the early morning sunshine. This Friday was starting off to be a gorgeous day.

It was time to check the weather of her dating life and see if it measured up. She returned to the kitchen and settled in front of her laptop. Clicking on the envelope icon, she quickly scanned the new e-mails in her inbox. She'd replied to FanningtheFlame's message after reading her profile about twenty times, writing:

Thanks for your beautiful message. It's good to know I'm not the only one out here who still believes in true love. Forgive my cynicism, but I sincerely hope your sentiments will be reflected in your actions as well as your words. If you think we'll be a good fit, let's set up a time to meet. Soon.

Mac figured her somewhat brief reply would scare off all but the truly willing. Spying an e-mail from her new admirer, she clicked it open.

> Cut to the chase, huh? Fine by me. I would be happy to show you I mean what I say and the sooner the better. Are you free this weekend? I hope so.

Well, she certainly didn't waste any time. *You wanted directness, didn't you?* she chided herself. Ignoring the tiny feeling inside crying out for her to stay within her comfort zone, Mac typed a reply quickly, before she could change her mind.

> Glad that's settled. I look forward to meeting you. I can't get away this weekend, but how about Wednesday night? We can meet at Dario's and go from there. Say 7:00 p.m.?

After hitting the Send button, Mac started to close the lid of her laptop but stopped when she heard the familiar ping announcing she had new mail. FanningtheFlame was online and confirmed their date.

Mac wondered if the hollow feeling in her gut was excitement or dismay.

"Hey, Haley, is Megan home?" Jordan stood in the doorway of her friends' brownstone duplex. For a reason she couldn't put her finger on, she hadn't wanted to go home after finishing up at the hospital. After making sure all her admitted patients were settled in for the night, she'd driven around aimlessly until she found herself at Megan and Haley's Oak Lawn home.

"You just missed her," Haley said. "She got a call from a client and went running out the door." She searched Jordan's face. "She made dinner before she left, though. Wanna join me?"

"I don't want to barge in on you." Lack of confidence was definitely not Jordan's usual style, but she felt dead tired and out of sorts.

Haley must have discerned that something was off, as she grabbed Jordan's arm and pulled her in. "You don't look good. I think you need to eat."

Jordan followed Haley into the kitchen and accepted the ice-cold bottle of beer Haley thrust into her hand. She noted Haley was still wearing her Dallas Fire Department uniform and, with her compact muscular body, she looked good in it. Taking a stab at small talk, she asked, "What's for dinner?"

"Meat loaf, mashed potatoes, green beans, baby carrots, and blackberry cobbler for dessert."

"Wow, do you guys eat this much every night?" Jordan blurted out. "How in the world do you stay in such good shape?"

"No, smart ass, we don't eat like this every night. Megan decided to surprise me with all of my favorites."

"What's the occasion?"

"It's the anniversary of the day we first met." The usually stoic Haley let loose a tiny grin at this revelation.

"Oh." Jordan was embarrassed that she'd crashed this special evening for her friends. "Look, maybe I should go."

"Chill. Do you see Megan here? It's not like you're interrupting anything. She probably won't be back for hours. Now, have a seat and eat with me," Haley urged, motioning to a table featuring a candlelit setting for two.

"Are you mad at her for taking off?" Jordan asked as they sat down.

"Mad? No. Disappointed that she had to leave? Sure. It happens. Hell, I get called in on emergencies all the time. If we got mad at each other for things we can't control, we'd never make it."

"Do you think you will?"

"Will what?"

Picking at bits of food, Jordan asked, "Make it."

"Why? Got the hots for my wife?" Haley was teasing, but her serious tone caused Jordan to shoot upright.

"No! I mean, she's beautiful and all. Who wouldn't have the hots for her? But I don't. I mean, I don't think of her that way. She's my friend, nothing more. She's a great friend, but we don't have anything more than a friendship between us."

"Stop talking, Doc. I was kidding."

"Oh." Jordan sighed.

"You're not eating," Haley observed.

"I'm not hungry."

"Spill it. What's wrong?"

"Nothing. I think I'm overly tired."

"Too many late dates?" Haley baited.

Jordan abruptly stood and slammed her beer bottle down on the table. "For your information, I've been working my ass off. I'm tired of everyone thinking I'm a playgirl who spends every waking moment getting laid."

Quick strides closed the distance between them, and Haley pushed Jordan back into her chair. "Settle down. I wouldn't have asked you in here if I thought you were going to throw a fit. I was making conversation. Be civil and let's talk."

As Jordan decided whether to stay or go, she sized up her friend's lover. Though she'd always been a welcome member of the group, Haley usually kept her own counsel, merely observing the interplay of the others. Jordan had never gotten to know her very well. However, in all her years as a paramedic in Dallas, Haley must have seen things that would make the rest of them cringe and she was equally sure Haley had both the physical and emotional strength to make her sit and be civil.

"Yeah, okay. I'm sorry. I don't know what's wrong with me lately. I feel out of sorts. I wanted to talk to Megan about it in hopes she could dispense some of her psychological mojo and make me feel better."

"I'm all you've got right now. Let's hear what's bugging you. I may not have much mojo, but I can listen."

"I don't know what's wrong. This whole week's been off. Last Saturday night I had a date with this woman I met online. We had dinner and then a nightcap back at her place."

Haley nodded. "You had sex."

"Yes, we had sex. Good sex. So I saw her again, probably a mistake. And she's been dropping by and calling me ever since."

"And that's a problem because?"

"Because she was perfectly clear she wanted to meet for a good time, no strings attached. I mean, she was clear about wanting no commitment up front. Really clear."

"Now she's acting like she wants more. Gotcha. Is that the only thing that's got you off your game?"

"Well, no. Then I see Mac acting all starry-eyed about some woman who is absolutely not her type and I confront her about it and she acts as if it's none of my business if she gets hooked up with some frumpy broad."

"Whoa, back up a minute. You ran into Mac while she was out on a date?"

"I didn't run into her. I was looking for her and there she was sharing coffee and small talk with a Shirley Feeney look-alike."

"When was this?"

"Last Sunday morning. Why?"

"What were you doing stalking Mac on a Sunday morning only hours after leaving the fling?"

"I wasn't stalking her." Jordan was indignant. "Mac and I usually do something together Sunday morning. It's our time."

"Uh-huh."

"What?"

"Nothing. So, Mac's dating a loser. What else are you bugged about?"

Jordan paused. She didn't want to confess Thursday night's antics to Haley. Fact was, she didn't know her all that well. She was Megan's partner, now legally married spouse, in some countries at least. Her general impression was Haley was pretty no-nonsense and generally tight-lipped. She had a hard time picturing Haley and Megan together; Megan was expressive and Haley rarely spoke more than ten words at a time. On the other hand, she thought she could trust Haley to not only keep her confidence, but to withhold judgment.

"I had a weird thing happen to me last night. I was in bed with a beautiful woman. It was an ideal situation. *She* picked *me* up at Sue's. I didn't even know her name. But I got up and left before we even did anything. I'd never seen her before, but she knew about me. I was freaked out."

"What did she know?"

"That I'm a doctor. I like sex. I'll go home with a gorgeous woman at the drop of a hat."

"Don't take this the wrong way, but is that information secret?"

Jordan stared hard at Haley and saw nothing but sincerity

in her expression. Deciding she wasn't being provoked, she responded, "No. I guess not. I suppose it struck a nerve to have her assume she could have me from the moment we met. It made me wonder whether everyone thinks I'm easy."

As she verbalized her vulnerability, she glanced up to check Haley's reaction and was met with a gentle gaze. "Do you remember what Megan said when you and Mac were writing your profiles? About how you put on this show of being noncommittal to stop anyone from knowing you may actually like them?" Haley waited for an acknowledgment, and then continued, "Well, I agree. You do put on a show, but people who know you and care about you see right through it. I don't know what's happened to you in the past to make you hide your real feelings, but I've seen enough to know you're a caring person. When you find someone who cares about you, I hope you'll let your true feelings show."

Jordan averted her eyes to keep Haley from seeing the gathering mist. Haley's speech, long for her, dredged up long-buried emotions. Not ready for them to surface, she switched the discussion to Haley. "How did you know Megan was the one for you?"

"Well, it wasn't love at first sight. The first time I saw her she was in the ER with one of her patients. I'd brought in two kids covered in first-degree burns, hanging onto life by the thinnest of threads. I'm sure I was a dashing figure, covered in soot. I was on my way to the bathroom to clean up a little before heading back out to finish my shift. Megan was walking down the hall and she crashed right into me. I was pissed off and told her to watch where she was going."

"You didn't!"

"Oh yeah. I was an ass. It was a hard night and I didn't think those kids were going to make it. I used to be known for my quick temper, and that night I was in rare form."

"What did she do?"

Haley sighed. "She told me I looked like I could use a cold drink. Then she bought me a bottle of water from the vending machine."

Jordan laughed, recognizing Megan's levelheadedness with which she was familiar. "What happened then?"

"It's hard to stay mad at someone who's being reasonable, especially since it wasn't her I was mad at her anyway. I said thanks for the water and left."

"That's it? Where's the fairy-tale ending?"

"There's no fairy-tale ending, as you're fond of pointing out. The next week, I found out who she was and apologized for being rude. I asked her out. She said yes. And now we're married."

Jordan had never experienced the kind of certainty about a woman Haley and Megan seemed to have from day one. "You make it sound so easy."

"Well, the hard part was deciding to take a chance."

"How did you know she was the right person to take a chance on?"

"Gut instinct. Once you take the first scary step, the rest either falls into place or it doesn't. If it does, you know you made the right choice. If it doesn't, you learn some lessons and move on."

"Again, you make it sound so easy."

"Don't be scared to take the first step, Jordan. What's the worst thing that can happen?"

"Total ruin of my reputation." Jordan grinned.

"Exactly." Haley smirked back.

CHAPTER TEN

It was a perfect day for a backyard barbeque. Mac slowed the Jeep as she reached the small driveway in front of Jordan's building. The driveway was technically reserved for those delivering takeout, dry cleaning, and other such amenities to the residents. Spying Jordan, she turned in and backed around, glad she wouldn't have to find a parking space in the tiny garage beneath the building.

"What? No top down? What kind of road trip is this?" Jordan teased as she folded her limbs into the sporty Wrangler.

"You'll survive." Mac headed for the freeway. Her brother and his family lived in Frisco, and though Frisco was a mere seventeen miles north of Dallas, it was the equivalent of driving to Oklahoma. "Besides, we wouldn't want your hair to get messed up, would we?"

"I'd live." Jordan let her gaze travel the length of Mac's form, taking in every inch. Funny, Mac looked even sexier in shorts and a T-shirt than she did in evening wear. Maybe it was because the casual clothes showed off more of her tanned, sculpted skin. Ignoring the part of her that wondered why she was suddenly noticing these attributes, she declared, "You look fantastic."

Mac looked down at her lime green T-shirt, khaki cargo shorts, and chartreuse sandals, and asked, "Did you eat breakfast? Perhaps it's a lack of food that's causing you to see things. I call this style 'rumpled barbeque couture.' It's anything but fantastic."

"Beauty is in the eye of the beholder."

"Seriously, Jordan, did you eat?"

Jordan placed one hand on Mac's shoulder and the other on her knee, and leaned in. "I don't need to eat to know you look great, okay?"

Flustered at what she was surely mistaking for innuendo, Mac managed to eke out an "Okay" in reply before changing the subject. "What's in the package?"

Jordan raised her eyebrows. "Package?"

"The one you put in the back. You know, when you got in the car?" Jeez, Mac thought, what was with her today?

"Oh, that." Jordan withdrew her hands, aware of an unease in Mac's body. She felt bothered to think that her touch had caused the tense reaction. "A Spider-Man Super Soaker. No eight-year-old should be without one."

"Alice is going to kill you."

Jordan flashed a wicked grin. "But Marty will love it. What did you get Jeremy?"

"Spidey's Triple Blast Hover Jet, and *Amazing Fantasy* number fifteen."

"Are you sure the last item is for Jeremy?"

Mac rolled her eyes. "It's a comic book, silly. The first appearance of Spider-Man in a Marvel comic. It's a collector's item."

"What a relief. I was scared you'd taken an inappropriate detour to an adult toy store for Jeremy's gift, but instead you're giving him something to mourn once he's an adult."

"To mourn?" Mac cast her a puzzled look.

"He's eight. Do you seriously think he'll keep it in cellophane for the next twenty years?"

Mac laughed. "You're a mess."

"That's for sure." Jordan fiddled with the radio tuner, dialing quickly past Nellie Furtado's "Promiscuous" and settling on "Unwritten" by Natasha Bedingfield. Leaning back in the bucket seat, she shifted slightly to get a better view of her companion. "Mackenzie?" She hesitated as she broached a more serious topic. "I've been meaning to apologize for last Sunday."

"Did you forget how to form the words?" Mac's tone held dual layers of tease and hurt.

"I'm sorry I was such a jerk and I'm sorry I haven't said so," Jordan replied sincerely. "I have no right to tell you who you should or shouldn't date."

"Well, you're right about that." Mac started to say more, but then refrained from a sermon on the issue. "Let's make a deal. I won't make any disparaging remarks about your dates and you'll return the favor."

"It's a deal," Jordan agreed.

She stared absently out the window. If her future dates were with the woman she'd been thinking about constantly for the last two days, Mac would have nothing to criticize.

Marty, Alice, and Jeremy lived in a two-story red brick house on a street lined with two-story red brick houses. The primary distinguishing characteristic was the stenciled numerical address at the curb. Mac parked her Jeep out front.

The birthday boy himself answered the door and greeted Mac and Jordan with big hugs. "Aunt Mac, Aunt Jordan, come out back and see what I got for my birthday."

Mac called out, "Brother dearest, what in the world did you buy this child?

"I'm not a child. I'm eight years old."

"Hey, partner, do you know any kids who might like to unwrap some presents?" Jordan asked, nodding toward the brightly colored packages in her arms.

"Me! Me!"

Marty walked into the foyer and snatched up his exuberant son, throwing him over his shoulder. With the same blond hair, brown eyes, and athletic build, Marty and Mackenzie were easy to pick as brother and sister. The slightly taller sibling addressed the child dangling from his shoulder. "Whoa there, mister. It's not time for presents yet. We have to feed the present bringers first." Turning to the women, he said, "Everyone's out back. Burgers and dogs go on the grill in fifteen minutes."

Jeremy grabbed a hand each from Mac and Jordan and led them quickly through the house, heading straight for the backyard. A dozen similarly excited eight-year-olds were dividing their time between the shallow end of a large swimming pool and what was clearly Jeremy's favorite birthday present, a trampoline.

Jordan added their gifts to the pile already amassed on one of the tables on the deck, remarking to Mac, "We may as well throw these in the trash. Our pitiful gifts have no chance against that monstrosity."

"Seriously," Mac agreed. "I had no idea we'd be up against that kind of competition. You want a beer?"

"Sounds great. Should we go see if Alice needs anything?"

"I'll get our beer and check with her on my way back. Don't hog the trampoline while I'm gone."

"I'll resist the impulse to show off," Jordan promised. As

she watched Mac head back into the house, she added quietly, "Especially if you're not going to be watching."

Mac paused in the doorway and looked back, puzzled by Jordan's mood. She sure was acting funny today. If Mac didn't know better, she'd think Jordan was flirting with her. Shrugging the thought aside, she made her way to the kitchen and greeted her sister-in-law with a quick hug around the shoulders.

Alice was up to her elbows in platters of burgers, hot dogs, and all the fixings. Without glancing up, she said, "Will you grab the bottles of ketchup and mustard in the fridge and put them in those thingies over there?" She waved in the direction of a stack of chrome condiment carriers sitting on the kitchen island.

"Sure," Mac responded, grabbing the bottles. "You have quite a crowd out there. What else do you need done?"

"I know it doesn't look like it, but everything is pretty well under control. We decided to keep it simple. The kids don't care what they eat. All they want to do is swim and play on the trampoline."

"And what a trampoline it is. I could have used a little warning so I could at least have tried to compete in the gift department."

"It was Marty's idea. Frankly, I think it's kind of dangerous, but he insisted the kids are as likely to hurt themselves in the pool. Now we have two death traps in the backyard." Alice grinned. "We should be the most popular house on the block."

"Are you going on about the trampoline again, woman?" The rumble of a deep male voice beat its owner into the kitchen.

"Get in here, Marty, and make yourself useful," Alice called out.

Mac laughed as her brother poked his head around the corner, checking out the situation before he approached. "Do you think she'll ever forgive me for making our son the happiest kid in the world?" he asked her.

"Quit trying to get everyone on your side, Marty." Alice shoved a plate of hamburger patties into his arms. "Start cooking and I'll let you know when you have redeemed yourself."

"Hang on a minute." Marty set the platter on the counter. "I need to perform a brief interrogation of my sister, the online dating guru." At Mac's loud groan, he said, "Don't worry. I already brought Alice up to date. You should know we have no secrets. Tell us everything. Have you been fishing lately?"

"I've declined the advances of a certain avid fisherwoman."

"And here I was hoping to host a fish fry for the two of you to celebrate your newfound happiness," Marty gibed.

Mac made a gagging gesture. "You will, however, be pleased to know I do have a bona fide date set up for next week."

"Someone you met online?" Alice asked.

"That's right. She said all the right things, so I decided to go ahead and set up a meeting and find out firsthand if she's for real."

"Good plan, sis. I hope she's fantastic." Sweeping her into a big hug, Marty added, "You deserve the best."

"Thanks, Marty." As Mac leaned into his embrace she whispered in his ear, "You do too."

"Marty, offer your sister a beer, then get your butt outside and start cooking."

"Damn," Mac muttered. "I told Jordan I'd be right back with something to drink."

"She's fine," Marty said. "We have coolers outside to keep the adults well hydrated. Someone will show her the stash."

"Cool. Well, brother dear, I think you better start grilling before your wife disowns you. I'll help. I do own one of the best restaurants in Dallas, you know."

"Yeah, kinda makes me wonder why we didn't put you in charge of this shindig. Come on and show me what you got." Marty retrieved his platter and led the way to the door.

❖

"Want to help me find the adult beverages?"

Jordan turned toward the sound of a silky voice and found herself looking at a gorgeous face framed in waves of light nut brown hair. Spicy amber and rose notes emanated from the woman, and the scent rallied her attention. She glanced toward the patio doors, but Mac was nowhere in sight. "Sure," she replied. "I could use something to help me cool off."

The beauty led her toward the deck, where picnic tables were lined with red and white checkered tablecloths. Several were stacked with plates and condiments. Off to the side several coolers were tucked under a bench, moisture glistening from the sides of their chrome frames. The spicy-scented woman leaned down to open one of the lids, then spent a moment sorting through the ice. Jordan's gaze was transfixed as her newfound friend's shorts rose up on her bronzed thighs to reveal the taut, round curves of her butt. At the same time, they rode down on her waist to show off the sculpted small of her back.

Jordan glanced away quickly as she was handed a frosty cold bottle of Harp Lager.

"Does this work?" the woman asked, still grasping the bottle.

"This works fine, thanks."

"My name is Samantha, by the way." She released Jordan's

bottle and waved toward the pool. "My son Adam is a friend of Jeremy's."

Jordan's thoughts raced. This bronze beauty was a mom—a hot mom, but a mom. She chided herself for feeling anything anyway. She didn't even know this woman and here she was getting all hot and bothered over a five-minute encounter that boiled down to some kid's mom helping her find a beer. Thrown, she considered the fact that she'd had her mind on Mac since the other night and had been seriously questioning her own MO. Was it realistic to think she could change? Her reaction to a total stranger at an eight-year-old's birthday party suggested an uphill battle.

"And your name is..."

Jordan realized that she hadn't replied to Samantha's introduction and fumbled to respond. "I'm Jordan, Jordan Wagner. I guess I'm like your son Adam. I'm here because I'm a friend of Jeremy's."

"Well, it's nice to meet you, Jordan Wagner. Any friend of Jeremy's is a friend of mine." Samantha punctuated this declaration by giving Jordan's hand a tight squeeze.

Jordan drew back from the grasp, resisting her proclivity to respond to the advances of a beautiful woman. "I should check and see if Alice needs anything."

"Totally unnecessary. If I know Alice, she has everything completely under control. I, however, could use some assistance if you don't mind." Samantha shrugged her shoulders, drawing down the sleeves of her gauzy white top. "I tried extra hard this morning, but I can't seem to get sun block on the spot right between my shoulders. Be a dear and rub it on for me."

Jordan's stare gave equal time to the well-toned bronzed shoulders and the bottle of sun block Samantha thrust in her hand. It didn't appear she had a choice in the matter. Slowly she flicked the cap open and angled the bottle toward her palm.

A slight squeeze brought creamy white liquid to the bottle's surface.

"Aunt Jordan, this is my friend Adam," Jeremy announced over Jordan's shoulder. "He wants to show me what he got me for my birthday. Could you move over a little bit?"

Jordan grinned at the interruption and quickly scooted over. "Sure, buddy. Nice to meet you, Adam. In fact, you arrived in the nick of time. Your mom needs some help." Jordan squirted a liberal dose of sun block into one of the boy's hands and placed the bottle on the table. "Now, you'll want to make sure you rub it in good, right there between her shoulders. We don't want your mommy to get burned."

Samantha glanced back at her, clearly vexed at the exchange. "Mommy's already suffering a little burn."

"I think you'll be fine. I'm going to head inside. Enjoy the party." Jordan stood and almost crashed into Mac, who was approaching with a tray of burger patties. "Hey, you. I was on my way to find you. Whatever happened to that beer you promised?"

Mac glanced down at the sweaty beer bottle in Jordan's hand and replied tersely, "Looks like you found a drink all on your own."

"Oh, yeah. Well, you were gone a long time and I found some coolers packed full of beer out here." Jordan was confused by the tone of her friend's response and wondered if she had misunderstood their conversation earlier. No, she thought, Mac clearly said that she was going inside to look for drinks. "Did I do something to make you mad?"

Mac sighed thinking about the tableau she'd witnessed moments earlier. Two, tall, gorgeous women leaning in close, sharing what was obviously an intimate moment. She'd seen the way the other woman devoured her best friend with hungry glances. Heck, she'd practically licked her lips as her hand slid over Jordan's, holding on as if to stake a claim. Mac wasn't sure why Jordan's flirtations were bothering her lately, but she didn't want to spend her nephew's birthday party watching another seduction.

"I'm not mad," she said coldly. "It doesn't do any good to get frustrated with things that are never going to change."

"I have no idea what you're talking about," Jordan protested.

"It doesn't matter. Everything's fine. Come help me get these on the grill." Mac led the way, grateful for the interruption the boys had provided to the action starting on the patio. Why was it that everyone thought Jordan was theirs for the taking?

Her thoughts were interrupted by a shout from Marty, who was balancing a platter of hot dogs, several packages of buns, and a wide selection of grilling implements. Jordan dashed over to save the platter as it was about to slip from his grasp.

"I figure we can feed the kids first and then we adults can have a semi-peaceful meal," he said as he lined the meat on the grill like a backyard barbeque master.

Jordan peered over his shoulder, admiring his skill. "Marty, who all is at this shindig?"

"Mostly kids from the neighborhood and their parents. I saw Samantha Bennett had you cornered. Care to share?"

Stealing a look at Mac, who was fiddling with the burgers, Jordan countered his question with one of her own. "What's her story?"

"I was hoping you'd tell me. She lives down the street in the biggest house on the block. She had a husband when she moved in, but he's been AWOL for the last few months. She seemed to be warming up to you. Maybe she's switching teams."

Fed up with what she was hearing, Mac interjected, "Big brother, you scare me when you try to act hip."

"I'm trying to encourage a little affection between friends. It seemed like she was into Jordan."

"Yeah, and who isn't." Mac's mutter was barely loud enough to register, but she caught a sharp look form Jordan.

Marty didn't notice, asking, "Jordan, what do you think about Mac's new prospect?"

"Prospect?" Jordan shot another look at Mac, who averted her eyes. "Gee, Marty, I don't seem to be privy to this latest piece of gossip. Dish."

"It's nothing," Mac said. "I was telling Marty about our online adventure and he thinks I should try harder to find love in cyberspace, that's all."

A burst of cold air from the house was followed by a parade of Mac and Marty look-alikes, alerting the guests that the rest of the Lewis clan had arrived.

Marty waved from his post at the grill. "Grab something to drink and send the kids over. We'll get them served and then I'll throw on food for us old folks."

CHAPTER ELEVEN

"Marty, Alice, everything tastes great." Jordan rubbed her stomach. "I'm going to have to put in extra miles on the bike tomorrow."

"Please. You look fantastic." Samantha had managed to snare a seat on Jordan's right. "I bet you could eat my cake and yours and still not gain an ounce."

Jordan's comeback was interrupted by a shout from the pool. "Mom, watch me, watch me!"

Samantha placed her hand across her brow, squinting against the sun while trying to focus on her energetic eight-year-old. "I'm watching, honey."

Running down the diving board, Adam yelled, "Look!"

His enthusiastic command caused most of the heads at the adult table to turn. But Jordan was still looking at Samantha's face, and the next few seconds were eerie as she watched fear unfold.

"Adam!" Samantha leapt to her feet and ran toward the pool.

Mac was already in the water, having anticipated the accident the moment she saw Adam jump into the air. The misplaced dive that followed caused him to strike his head on the diving board, and he was floating in the deep end, a small trail of blood nearby. Jordan ran to the side of the pool, pulling while Mac pushed the youngster onto the stone border. Samantha tried to push them both away as she dropped down at the prone boy's side.

Mac gently grasped her shoulder. "Jordan's a doctor. Give her a little space."

Samantha nodded, tears flowing. Though she stopped trying to elbow Jordan aside, she remained next to her, sobbing. Unbearable moments of silence passed as Jordan listened to Adam's chest, then turned him on his side.

"Is he going to be okay?" Samantha begged.

At that very moment, Adam gasped and spit up a healthy dose of pool water. Jordan wiped his chin with the tail of her shirt and examined him carefully. He had a gash on his forehead and a busted lower lip. Both required stitches and, damn it, she didn't have her bag. Several years in the trauma ward during her fellowship had taught her injuries requiring quick attention were apt to occur anyplace at any time. As a result, she kept a medical bag packed and ready in the trunk of her Beemer, which wasn't with her today since they had ridden in Mac's Jeep.

Leaning in so only the little boy could hear her, she asked, "Adam, can you hear me?"

She barely caught his whimpered, "Yes."

"Good. Do you remember who I am?"

He nodded. "You're Jeremy's aunt."

She smiled. "You're going to be okay, but I want to take you to the hospital where we can check you out. You okay with that?" She looked back over her shoulder and was nose to nose with the boy's hovering mother. "Samantha, is your car here or at your house?"

"We walked here. Should I go get it?"

Several voices piped up, offering to drive. Jordan looked up from the mother and son and realized all the party guests were gathered around. "You've got an SUV, right?" she asked Marty.

He dragged out his keys. "I'll carry him."

Jordan nodded. "Someone toss me a towel and let's get this show on the road."

❖

About two hours later, Jordan finally returned to the waiting room. "Sorry for the wait. They're stitching him up now. His X-rays came back fine."

"Thank goodness." Mac sighed.

"Where is everyone?"

"Marty went back home." The adults had decided it was unfair to Jeremy to end to his birthday on such a horrible note, so the party was continuing in a subdued fashion. "How are you doing?"

"I'm fine. I'm not the one whose son almost broke his neck."

"Well, I bet Samantha is impressed with the heroic figure you cut," Mac said. "Lucky you were there to sweep her off her feet and save the day."

"Leave it alone, Mac. Her only concern right now is her little boy. She's worried he's going to have a scar, which he probably will."

"I'm sure you can fix that too," Mac said sweetly.

Jordan's face tightened. "Adam may not want to lose his chance at a bona fide scar. He thinks it'll be cool. Can you believe a couple of hours ago he was unconscious and now he thinks his brush with death was cool?"

Mac smiled. "Are they letting him go home now?"

"Yes. He'll be sore, but they've decided not to keep him overnight."

"I'll call Marty. He's offered to give them a ride home." Mac hesitated. "Are you staying?"

"No. I've done all I can."

Mac bit back the reply that hovered. Jordan's flat tone and blank expression suggested she'd been teased enough. "Now that all the excitement is over, I'm starving."

"I wonder why. You left a perfectly good hot dog to go for a swim."

"It's hard to pass up a chance to be the hero of the party. Even for a hot dog. Though you did kind of show me up with all your doctor mumbo jumbo."

"Sorry. Next time, I'll let you do the heavy breathing."

"Very funny." Mac smiled. "What do you say we get something to eat?"

"Sure, but nowhere fancy, okay? I have blood on my shirt."

Mac grimaced. Sliding her hand into Jordan's, she said, "You know, you did save the day. Adam definitely thinks you're a hero."

"Impressing kids isn't always so easy."

"Unlike their mothers." Mac expected a comeback, but Jordan's hand slid away and she stood, her expression weary.

"Let's get out of here." She started for the door, not even waiting to see if Mac was following.

Disconcerted, Mac jumped up and strode after her. When they got to the car, she said, "There's an extra T-shirt in my gym bag if you want to change. I was thinking we could grab a burger at Hunky's."

"That sounds like a plan." Jordan let herself into the passenger side.

She was silent as they drove, but her discomfort showed in every shallow breath she drew. Mac knew her too well not to notice, but she also knew enough not to speak. Whatever Jordan had on her mind, she wasn't going to share it.

❖

Parking on the Cedar Springs strip was scarce, but Mac found a place for the Jeep on a residential street a couple of blocks away and they walked in silence to the popular neighborhood burger joint. The diner itself wasn't busy, as most of the evening crowd in Oak Lawn had already eaten and were on their way out to the bars. Mac and Jordan settled into a booth and wasted no time ordering cheese burgers, fries and draft beer.

Mac grinned as she watched her fidget. Jordan's full chest strained against the cotton fabric of the tight little T-shirt she'd borrowed. Truth be told, she looked damn good. The taut garment accented both well-toned muscles and ample breasts.

"What's the matter?" Mac gazed down pointedly. "A little tight?"

"More than a little. Now I remember why I stopped raiding your closet back in high school. Of course, this is pretty tight." Jordan's smile didn't quite reach her eyes. "It must be your 'impress the girls at the gym with your toned body' shirt."

"Yeah, that's it. But now you've stretched it out with your big boobs, it won't impress anyone anymore."

"Very funny."

"That's me, the good humor girl."

"Speaking of being in a good humor, Marty seemed to think you're excited about an upcoming date. Care to dish?"

"Poor segue. Marty wants me to be happily married, so he thinks every date is the first step down the aisle."

"Poor dodge," Jordan countered. "Do you have a date with someone new?"

"Maybe."

"What do you mean 'maybe'?" Jordan cocked her head at the cagey response.

"I have a date, but I don't want to talk about it."

"Oh, is it with that Charla woman again? I swear I won't make fun, though I don't get what you see in her."

Mac sighed with frustration. "No, Jordan, it's not with Charla. It's with someone new. I don't want to talk about it."

"You mean you don't want to talk about it with *me*." Jordan's voice rose. "You had no problem discussing your newfound love with Marty."

Mac kept her tone even despite the defensiveness Jordan's accusation sparked. "He asked and I told him I have a date. I told you what I told him. End of story."

"Did you meet this new love interest online?"

"Can we change the subject?"

Jordan's response dripped sarcasm. "Sure, Mac. Let's talk about whatever it is people who haven't known each other practically their whole lives talk about."

Mac rolled her eyes. "Don't be an ass."

"I share everything with you. I don't get why you're shutting me out."

"Maybe we'd both be better off if you didn't share everything."

"What's that supposed to mean?" Jordan's look reflected genuine surprise.

"Maybe we don't need to share every detail of our love, or in your case, sex lives with each other. We have plenty of other things to talk about." Even as she spoke the words, she wanted to take them back. They'd always shared everything, and it felt strange to have to back away.

Jordan stared across the table, stunned. Apparently, her commentary about Mac's last date had pissed Mac off. But surely Mac knew she only cared about her and didn't think Charla was worthy of her. She certainly didn't expect to be shut out like this and she didn't think it was fair. They'd shared the details of their dating lives for the last twenty years. There had to be something else going on, but Jordan couldn't fathom what it might be. Mixed in with her confusion over the wall Mac had erected were other confounding feelings. For the past few days, Jordan's thoughts had been laced with more than friendly feelings toward Mac, stirring butterflies in her stomach. Even now, Mac looked adorable in her still-damp shorts and T-shirt. Normally, Jordan would have sealed the deal with the likes of Samantha Bennett, regardless of the accident. She would have offered herself as a distraction, one the hot mom would have been unable to resist, not that she'd tried. She'd done everything she could to capture Jordan's attention.

Jordan toyed with her cutlery, sneaking covert looks at Mac as she consumed fries, seemingly oblivious. Whether her quest was for comfort or craving, she wasn't sure, but she couldn't look away. Her only certainty was she wanted something she had never experienced before.

"Jordan, did you hear what I said?" Mac's tone was exasperated.

Looking directly into her eyes, Jordan saw pleading beneath the exasperation. Mac was pleading with her to be given this, whatever it was. Maybe independence. She started to reply, but self-realization stopped her. She had no business saying anything about what she felt when she didn't know what it meant, for either of them. Noting Mac was waiting for a response, she said simply, "Yes. You're right. There's plenty of other stuff we can talk about."

"Okay. Well, thanks, then. I appreciate your understanding."

Jordan's gaze didn't waver. "Whatever you need, Mac. Whatever you need."

They finished their meal without another word, despite the "plenty of other stuff" they could talk about.

CHAPTER TWELVE

She'd been waiting in the bar mere moments when the woman approached. Prompt—she liked that. *Looks even better than her photo. Bonus.* So far, things were going well.

"Mackenzie?" The voice, questioning at first, turned quickly to a silky purr. "Your picture does you no justice. You're gorgeous."

Mac knew only one other person who was as forward, and it had taken years for her to grow used to it. She fought to hide a bashful response, choosing to appear equally confident. "Thanks Rebeca. You look terrific yourself." Indicating the hostess stand nearby, she asked, "Would you like to have a drink here or go ahead and get a table in the dining room?"

"Let's get a table, better for private conversation."

"Great. We have a reservation. I'll let them know we're here." Mac made her way to the hostess. While she exchanged words with her, she glanced over her shoulder. Her attempt to observe her date discreetly was thwarted by her date's seeming attempt to do the same. Their eyes locked. Mac was the first to glance away, but not without noticing Rebeca take a sweeping survey, head to toe. A bold grin signaled her approval and Mac's face grew warm in response.

Their table was in a small alcove situated in a perfect spot, removed from the front door and the kitchen, secluded and intimate. Leaving their menus unopened, they chatted for a few minutes. The conversation revolved around the basics.

Upon discovering Mac was a restaurateur, Rebeca expressed surprise at her choice of location for their first date. "Why not invite me to the Lakeside? Then you could have been on your home turf and you could be sure that the food would be great. It always is."

"Thanks. You've been there before?"

"Of course. You must know that you have a big following in the community."

"Sure. I'm surprised I haven't seen you there."

"I must have been in when you were busy, or on your day off. It's a great place." Rebeca paused to take a drink of water. "I'm a bit surprised you chose this restaurant. It hasn't been open very long. In fact, I don't know anyone who's tried it yet."

Mac leaned in close and in a low voice said, "Rebeca, I have a confession to make."

Emerald eyes signaled anticipation. "I love confessions."

"I'm mixing business with pleasure." Mac paused. "This place offers a menu very similar to the Lakeside and I wanted to check out the competition. I figured I could try two new things at the same time. Hate me?"

Rebeca laughed. "Not in the least. You have a very practical side. Good to know. We may as well make the most of this, don't you think? What's your usual modus operandi when you're checking out the competition?"

"I usually order a little bit of everything. Then, either the waiter thinks I'm a huge pig, or they mistake me for a restaurant critic. The latter usually results in better service, but I try never to give them a hint either way."

"As good a shape as we're both in, I think there's little danger that we'll be mistaken for huge pigs. Let's make this a working date, then, shall we?"

Mac nodded, pleased at the response. This was going to be fun.

A couple of hours later, they contemplated each other across a French press brimming with dark roast coffee. The waiter's only remark during the constant parade of dishes had been something along the lines of "perhaps next time you would like a larger table," but his observation was delivered with a smile.

Though she had a few criticisms with regard to several of the dishes, Mac decided this establishment would be a worthy rival to the Lakeside. Checking out her date, she asked, "Are you as full as I am?"

"God, yes. I can't believe you ordered four desserts. I see extra hours in the gym in my future."

"Do you have a full gym where you work?" Rebeca had said she worked for a physical therapy facility, but she'd been short on the detail.

"Of course we do. Well, it's not exactly at my work. We have privileges at Images and I use them liberally."

Mac ventured a bold response. "I can tell."

"Why, Ms. Lewis, you are kind. Thanks for noticing."

"I've been meaning to check Images out. A friend of mine knows a personal trainer there. I go to the Y occasionally, but I could use the discipline of a training routine."

Rebeca didn't pick up on the prospect of a workout companion. "I remember your profile said you're a cyclist. I'm sure you get all the exercise you want that way. You're in great shape."

"Well, then thanks back to you for noticing, Ms. Blixen. With the Lakeside close to the trails, cycling is the easiest way for me to keep in shape. I keep both my bikes at the restaurant so I can take off whenever I get a break."

"You must spend a lot of time at work."

"Nature of the beast. Luckily it's a great place to hang out. My friends call it their home away from home. And actually, if it wasn't for them, I wouldn't be sitting here. Going online was their idea. The perfect dating solution for a workaholic like me."

"Has the experience been successful for you?"

Mac reflected on her "date" with Charla and e-mails with the likes of the fisherwoman. She realized these would make funny stories one day, but she wasn't ready to laugh about her exploits. She thought about sharing Jordan's success as an anecdote of the wonders of electronic matchmaking, but loyalty prevented her from intruding on her best friend's privacy. It wasn't like Jordan practiced any discretion, and frankly, her one-night stands didn't add up to success in Mac's book. But she still wasn't ready to discuss a close friend with this complete stranger.

A gentle voice prodded her out of her musings. "Hey, Laker Gal? Are you ready to call it a night?"

Mac snapped back to the conversation. "Oh, gosh, I'm sorry. I think I fell into a food coma. Usually, I try to eat like a lady on at least the first few dates and wait until much later in the relationship before I reveal myself as a foodaholic."

"Would you like to give this another try?"

Mac paused. She felt cautious about rushing into a series of dates destined to climax with the combining of households, but the evening had been pleasant and Rebeca was beautiful. She wasn't proposing, and she never would if Mac always took this long to answer her questions. Fumbling her way out of rambling thoughts, she finally responded, "I'd love to."

"Great. I'll give you a call."

❖

Ten Tips for Online Dating. *Let me guess*, Mac said to the screen. *Don't eat all the food on earth on your first date. Save some in case she decides she wants to see you again.* An hour after arriving home, she'd given up on the possibility that her indigestion would cure itself and had taken an antacid. Settling at the table with a tall glass of water, she noticed the new mail icon displayed on her laptop. Rebeca, no doubt, writing a Dear Huge Pig letter: At first I thought you were cute, but then you ate the entire city of Dallas in one sitting. When I said I wanted to see you again, I didn't mean you had to make yourself big enough I could see you across town.

Actually, Rebeca seemed to have had a good time and Mac had too. Maybe she would actually call. Of course, these were modern times. Mac didn't have to sit around waiting for women to call her. She signed onto the TLL site and glanced at the pop-up bar to see who else was signed on. She was a little disappointed and surprised to find Jordan wasn't present. A part of her wanted to share the details of her evening, but Aimee's words of caution echoed and she reaffirmed her decision to keep this new venture under wraps for now.

Grinning, she started typing a "had a great time" message to Rebeca. She wrote and rewrote, struggling with what should be such a quick and easy task. The very act of sending a message seemed a little too eager, and she wasn't eager. In fact, she was feeling inexplicably reticent. Unable to put her finger on what was holding her back, she took one last look to see if Jordan had signed on. Her absence decided the question. She deleted the message to Rebeca, unsent, and went to her bedroom to read a few pages from *Lost Loves* before falling asleep.

The revelation lay like a land mine between them and both feared to tread the hazardous path back to the other. Shannon drew into herself, seeking healing for the wound inflicted on her vulnerable soul. *Why,* she cried silently, *why did I speak my feelings? I barely know this woman.*

This fact was made plain by the proclamation uttered from her lover's lips. "I will never say I love you. I will never be in love with you or anyone, for that matter."

The words were not couched in sentimental phrasing, but instead landed like rocks thudding on the soil, ruining the garden Shannon had prepared for the growth of their future together. She posed a simple question, hoping the answer would carry the rocks away. "Why?"

"I don't believe in love. I do like you immensely and I thoroughly enjoy what we have together. Can't that be enough?"

Why should it have to be? Shannon's inner voice screamed. Her outer voice formed rational questions. "I don't understand. Where do you draw the line between 'immense like' and love? What are you trying to tell me?"

Dylan paused before delivering a careful response. "I will never make a life commitment to you, never pledge you undying depth of feeling. I don't want those things from you or anyone and I don't expect or want them for myself."

Shannon sat still unable and unwilling to respond for fear of what might follow. Frozen with disbelief, she held back tears. She had no desire to let this woman, who now seemed a stranger, witness her vulnerabilities any longer. Base instincts led her to reach for the nearest garment and cover her bare breasts. Suffering from the overexpense of feeling, she could not afford to be naked anymore.

A burning desire to know what Shannon would do next wasn't enough to keep Mac's eyes open. She fell asleep with the book still clutched in her hand.

❖

"Aimee tells us you had a date with someone new last week," Megan said.

"Actually, I saw her again yesterday," Mac replied, looking toward the bike trail. There was still no sign of Jordan. Everyone was relieved, since they would be able to discuss the details of her birthday party without having her walk up on them. "We had lunch at the Bronx."

"Are you going to tell us all about it or are we going to have to hold you down and torture you until you talk?"

Mac reflected on her two dates with Rebeca. She supposed they'd had a good time getting to know each other, but something was off and she wasn't sure if they were getting to know each other after all. Rebeca seemed evasive whenever Mac mentioned her job. Career usually provided fertile ground for conversation topics, so it was strange that she dodged career questions. And she always steered the conversation to Mac's friends, expressing a strange interest in all they did. When Jordan's name was mentioned, she acted like a reporter hot on the trail of a breaking story. Mac had spent the last week trying to reconcile the intelligent, together woman from their first date with the evasive, yet inquisitive woman who'd since emerged.

Realizing she hadn't responded to Megan's question and unsure about how to relay what were probably nothing more than initial dating jitters, Mac merely shrugged and answered, "What can I say? She's attractive and fun to be around. We seem to be getting along fine."

"Fine, huh? I've always considered the word 'fine' to be a nice substitute for 'dull.'"

"What are we talking about?" A bag landed on the floor and Jordan pulled out a chair.

Mac glanced around the table, willing her friends into silence, wondering how much of their conversation Jordan had heard on her approach. Deciding she couldn't have heard much, she replied, "Nothing important. Nice of you to join us."

"Sorry I'm late. I had to check on a patient. What's got you all looking so twitchy?" She cocked her head as everyone looked to the others to respond.

Megan spoke first. "Nothing much." She poked Haley in the side as if to signal she should chime in with a more informative response. Haley gave her a startled look and said nothing.

Jordan obviously thought the whole exchange was amusing. "You're trying to decide what to get me for my birthday."

Mac scrambled for a response that wouldn't give their plans away. "Yep, we are. Glad you're here to give input. I was thinking a Learjet, but these gals think you wouldn't get enough use out of it."

She cast a desperate glance at Aimee, who promptly added, "I personally think we should get you a real house, a sprawling estate in Highland Park. I would reduce my commission, of course."

Megan picked up the string and ran with it. "A new wing

for your practice, complete with the spa amenities you've been talking about. You could name it after us, put a plaque on the wall."

Jordan laughed and started to take her seat when her BlackBerry buzzed. "Those are all great suggestions. I have to take this call, but I'll be right back with some suggestions of my own."

As Jordan walked away from the table, Mac sighed. "How lame are we at surprises? One idle question and we almost gave it all away."

"We recovered nicely and I'm sure she doesn't have a clue," Megan said. "Now, let's talk about something else in case we don't see her coming back. Everything will go off without a hitch, I'm sure of it."

CHAPTER THIRTEEN

When the shouting died down, Jordan was finally able to focus on the sea of faces all staring at her. The usual suspects—Megan, Haley, Aimee—were present, along with the entire staff of the Lakeside. She spotted several members of her local LGBT networking group, all the members of her office staff, and a few doctor friends. Someone must have swiped her BlackBerry to make the guest list. This was quite a crowd. Sally Gannon stood in front of her saying something, but Jerry Lee Lewis was wailing the lyrics of "Thirty-nine and Holding" and Jordan was reduced to trying to lip-read.

She nodded when Sally mouthed, "Scotch?"

Sally made her way to the bar, and Jordan watched her engage in a similar exercise to accomplish her purpose. Sally always wore a basic "uniform" of khakis and polo or button-down shirts in muted colors and brown or black Doc Martens. Her close-cropped hair remained in the same style and she wore no jewelry except a simple stainless steel watch and a plain gold band on her left ring finger. Jordan liked her and appreciated all she did to make Mac's life easier.

Mac, Megan, Aimee, and Haley crowded around Jordan, exchanging hugs and exclamations.

"You should've seen your face," Megan shouted above the music. "Who would've believed you would be easy to trick?"

"You were surprised, weren't you?" Mac asked.

Jordan laughed. "I'm sure I looked stunned. I had no idea y'all were up to anything. You got me." She slipped an arm around Mac's waist, leaned in close, and whispered in her ear, "This was quite a surprise, Miss Lewis."

"Don't look at me. This was a group effort." Gesturing to the rest of the group, she continued, "Everyone here gets equal blame, uh, I mean credit. Now, it's time for the good doctor to make the rounds and greet her guests." She pushed Jordan gently toward the crowd.

Jordan felt an overwhelming desire to stay right where she was, but Mac was right, she was obliged to circulate. She kissed her on the cheek, whispered, "Thanks for all of this," and moved reluctantly away.

As she made her way around the restaurant, she was impressed with every detail of the party. Paper lanterns in a rainbow of colors brightened the room, and the tables were adorned with glass vases filled with colorful gerbera daisies. Servers wandered the room urging guests to partake of a host of scrumptious appetizers, and a large table near the doors to the Dock was covered with more of the tempting treats. A deejay spun pure 1980s retro. Thinking there would be dancing later, Jordan paused to speak to various groups of her friends, colleagues, and acquaintances, sampling the goodies along the way.

About forty-five minutes later, having made her way back to where she started, she spotted another familiar face and wondered how she could have missed seeing Grace in her earlier pass through the crowd. The tall brunette was standing with her back to the bar, lined with guests vying for beverages. Jordan waded through the crowd to say hello.

Grace's eyes lit up when she saw her, and she waved a greeting. At the same time, a man standing next to her turned slightly, placing a drink in her hand. The light from the bar illuminated his profile as he placed an arm across Grace's shoulders and nuzzled against her neck. The smile on Grace's face turned quickly into a grimace as Jordan stopped walking, immobilized. As Grace started toward her, she forced herself to move. Ignoring looks from the guests she passed, she dashed from the room, not stopping until she reached the back corridor of the restaurant.

Crouching, she bent over and tried to catch her breath. Her head was spinning and the pit of her stomach ached. The sour taste in her mouth signaled nausea, and dizziness made her sink to the ground. Questions pelted her like hail, striking hard and often. Why was her father here? Why was he kissing Grace? Why was Grace looking like she enjoyed it? How long has this been going on? Who else knew?

Rocking in place, Jordan felt small and vulnerable and betrayed.

❖

"Don't you dare come in here." Nick looked affronted. "We have everything under control and you'll mess up my system. Go be a fabulous hostess."

"Fine, fine." Mac backed off. "I thought you might welcome a little help, but obviously I was wrong. I'll leave things to your capable hands."

"I will let you know if I need help, which I won't. Now go." Nick waved a knife and Mac hastily beat a path to the door running into an out-of-breath hostess.

"Looking for me?"

"Yes, ma'am." The young woman was obviously flustered and the words came tumbling out. "There's a lady by the bar. She wasn't on the guest list, but she said you meant for her to be here tonight. I asked her to wait while I checked with you, but she insisted."

Mac was puzzled, but decided if a party crasher was the only problem tonight, then things were going pretty smoothly. "No worries. Why don't you show the mystery guest to my office?"

Relieved, the young woman nodded and returned to the front of the restaurant while Mac went to her office to wait. At the sound of a knock, she called out, "Come on in."

Looking up at the woman walking confidently toward her, she was thrown to see it was Rebeca Blixen. There wasn't enough time to filter her initial reaction. "What the hell are you doing here?"

"Hello, Mackenzie. I take it you're not happy to see me."

Mac didn't know what she felt. Or rather, wasn't sure which of the various feelings she was experiencing was going to take precedence. Rebeca looked hot and she was dressed to the nines. Despite the delicious sight of the woman standing in front of her, Mac felt annoyance creep in. She had purposely not invited a date tonight. She and Jordan had been a little out of sorts lately and she wanted to recapture some of their former camaraderie with a girls' night out, no dates for either of them. Plus, she wanted the party to go off without a hitch, which meant expending her energy on hostess duties instead of dating niceties.

"Unhappy isn't the word."

"Mad?"

"I'm not mad," Mac said. "I'm confused about why you would show up here when I told you I had plans tonight."

"Maybe I wanted to grab a bite to eat." Rebeca sidled over to stand behind Mac's chair. Lightly kneading Mac's shoulders, she said softly. "I have quite an appetite."

"Come on, now. It's pretty obvious we have a private party going on. In fact, there's a guest list at the door."

"The waitress was very understanding when I told her you and I are dating."

"You did what?" Mac didn't try to hide her consternation at Rebeca's gall.

Rebeca swiveled Mac's chair so they were face-to-face and smiled a sultry smile. "Ease up. You're acting like I breached a government-secured facility."

❖

Jordan shook herself off and squared her shoulders, preparing to reenter the party when she heard voices down the hall. One of the voices was definitely Mac's and she sounded pissed. The other voice was fairly soft and hard to make out, but it sounded familiar. She could hear more as she walked softly toward Mac's office. Pausing outside the door, she found herself eavesdropping as she decided what to do.

"Well, I'm here now." This time the voice was unmistakable. Jordan nudged the door open a few inches, just in time to see Rebeca Blixen pout seductively and bend low over Mac. "It's a party. Will one more guest send it into a tailspin?"

"That's not the point." Mac sounded annoyed. "You shouldn't be here."

Infuriated, Jordan swung the door wide. "I think what Mac's trying to say is that she didn't want me to know she's dating you."

Mac jumped and twisted to face her. "Jordan, what are you doing back here?"

"Sorry, Mac." Jordan didn't bother to temper her sarcasm.

"I wasn't spying. I was looking for a friend, but I think I need to look elsewhere."

"I don't know what you're talking about." Mac stood and quickly moved past Rebeca. "Hey, birthday girl, let's head back up front."

Jordan shrugged her off, jerking her head in Rebeca's direction. "What about your date?"

"Oh, she's leaving. Jordan, this is—"

"Malibu," Jordan interjected, "nice to see you again."

Mac looked back and forth between each of the women standing in the room. "What's going on?" She stared at Jordan.

Jordan stared squarely back, her hazel eyes fire-flecked with anger. "I've already met your new girlfriend. Don't try to tell me you didn't know."

Mac turned to the other woman. "Rebeca?"

"Why, yes, dear, Dr. Wagner and I are already acquainted."

Mac didn't miss the innuendo dripping from Rebeca's response, and the craving in her eyes told her innuendo had been something more concrete on at least one occasion. Realization dawned and she spat her response. "Don't 'dear' me. I think it's time for you to leave. Past time, in fact."

Rebeca turned to Jordan. "Looks like I've worn out my welcome with your friend. Are you leaving? Can I give you a lift?"

"Oh, I'm leaving, all right, but not with you. Get out of my sight."

With a shrug, Rebeca strode over to Mac, pulled her close, and kissed her full on the mouth. She quickly regained her balance as Mac pushed her roughly away. With a wink at Jordan, she left the room.

"What the hell is going on here?" Mac demanded.

Jordan turned in surprise. "I should be asking you." Pointing to the departing Rebeca, she asked, "*She's* your new girlfriend? No wonder you didn't want to tell me."

"Why should you mind if I want to date one of your cast-offs?"

"I don't get why you're pissed at me. What did I do? So I dated her first. Do you think I might have ruined her for you?"

"Give me a break. You're jealous because I can get the same girls you can. All our lives, you've told me who I should and shouldn't date, and you've made sure you get the best ones for yourself. It must be killing you that Rebeca chose me."

"You think I'm jealous?"

"I think you're consumed with it."

Jordan channeled her fury into a penetrating stare. Despite her anger, she knew Mac was partly right. She *was* jealous, even consumed with it, but not for the reasons Mac thought. Her earlier plan to share her feelings with Mac over an intimate birthday dinner for two dissolved into images of Mac sharing intimate moments with Rebeca. Her anger deflated and sorrow settled in. All she wanted to do was leave, quickly. Her hand on the doorknob, she faced her best friend and willed herself to show no sign of her feelings. One final thought needed to be spoken.

"Mackenzie, you don't know me at all." She left the room without registering a response.

Spying the tall redhead stalking down the hallway, Nick rushed to Mac's office and entered without announcement. Mac was standing in the middle of the room, staring at the door.

"Nick, I need a minute."

"Sit down, Mac." As if he didn't trust her to follow his command, he pushed her gently onto the couch. "I heard."

Mac's eyes shifted downward and she shuffled in place.

"You're not embarrassed, are you? I can't believe that Blixen bitch had the gall to show up here tonight. I called the front and told Sally to make sure she was escorted out of the building and told never to darken these doors again."

Mac barely registered his words, but she felt comfort in his presence. "Nick, I think Jordan left the party."

"Are you mad at her?"

She could tell he genuinely wasn't sure. "I don't know what I feel right now. Maybe some anger mixed with something else. What am I going to tell everyone if the birthday girl isn't here?"

Nick hugged her close. "We'll say she ate lunch at that new place and contracted horrible food poisoning. We provide a plausible explanation for her absence and put the competition out of business at the same time." His grin was devilish.

Mac managed a smile in return and poked her friend in the ribs. "You're bad. Have I told you lately how much I appreciate you?"

"No time to be sappy. Get up." He pulled her to her feet. "You have guests who want to eat, drink, and be entertained. If you provide enough of all three, they'll forget they were here for a birthday party in the first place."

Mac knew he was right. She couldn't hide in her office all night, hoping against hope that the party guests wouldn't notice the hostess and guest of honor had both disappeared. Steeling herself, she followed Nick down the back hallway toward the bar. Pausing before the swinging half doors, she surprised herself with a brief touch of optimism. Maybe Jordan hadn't left after all. As frustrated as she was about their fight, she hoped her sweeping survey of the room would reveal the redhead. In her very core she knew, before she finished looking, Jordan was not in the room. No way would her proud friend have stuck around after the nasty exchange between them. She was probably on her way to Sue Ellen's right now, seeking solace for her ruined birthday. *Well*, she resolved, *I'll have to salvage things on my own.* Determined to make the best of the situation, Mac returned to the party, nearly jumping out of her skin at a touch to her shoulder.

"Mackenzie, have you seen Jordan?"

"Oh. Hi, Grace. I didn't know you were here. Actually, Jordan had to leave."

"Dammit. I should have talked to her before tonight. I should have known something like this would happen." Grace seemed to be talking more to herself than to Mac. At Mac's puzzled look, she said, "I brought Jacob. She saw us together and I think she misunderstood the context."

"A common problem tonight." Mac added with a whisper, "Jordan and I had a misunderstanding of our own. She's pretty angry and I think she left."

"Where do you think she went?"

Mac held back on announcing her theory, deciding her irritation at Jordan's departure didn't justify trashing her friend's reputation. Though Grace surely knew Jordan well enough to know she was most likely on her way to soak some of her woe in a bottle of Scotch.

"She's resourceful. Frankly, Grace, I don't care if it's her birthday. She was a jerk. I plan to tell everyone she was called to an emergency and I had one of the wait staff take her home. A blatant lie, but everyone may as well have fun since the party's in full swing. No sense letting all this hoopla go to waste."

Grace frowned. "I don't know, Mac. I think she's feeling very hurt right now. As impetuous as she is, I'm worried about leaving her to her own devices."

Mac shrugged. "I hear you, and I don't want Jordan to be

alone with her hurt, but I'm a little hurt myself." At Grace's questioning look, she responded, "I don't want to get into it. Look, I know her. She's probably on her way to a bar. She doesn't have her car. Probably the worst thing to happen to her will be a colossal hangover. Call her if you want, but I can't talk to her right now without risking some serious damage to our friendship."

"Who's damaging whose friendship?"

Mac and Grace both looked up to see Aimee and Megan approaching. The exchanged glance sealed a tacit agreement that Mac would be the one to respond. She deliberately ignored the original question and flashed a fake smile at her friends. "Hey chicks, having fun?"

Aimee responded, "Sure, but the guest of honor has slipped out and it didn't look like she was coming back. What's going on?"

Mac sighed. "The official story is she's responding to an emergency." She paused, thinking it wasn't entirely untrue that Jordan was responding to her own private emergency by running away. Bracing herself for the onslaught of questions from their friends, she said, "But the real story is Jordan and I had a fight right on the heels of her seeing Grace in what she thought was an intimate moment with her father."

She knew this last revelation wouldn't have the same impact for her friends as it did for her. They didn't know the history behind Jordan's tenuous relationship with her father, and she was too worn out by the drama of the night to fill them in.

"Is she okay?" Megan asked.

"I think she just wants some time alone," Mac said. "Tell you what. I need your help to make sure this party goes on as if nothing's wrong. We'll have brunch Sunday and I'll fill you in on all the details. I don't have the energy to process it all right now. Deal?"

Megan and Aimee nodded, obviously dying to know more, but resolving to wait for answers. Megan spoke first.

"Let's get you back to the party. Get everyone's attention and I'll announce Jordan had to leave, but we'll blow out the candles and cut the cake in her honor." Megan grabbed Mac's arm and steered her toward the bar. Aimee took up her post on Mac's other side and Mac relaxed into the solid support of her friends.

The rest of the evening was a blur. Haley and Megan, at Nick's instruction, drove Mac home. He promised to make sure her Jeep made it home sometime before morning. After a blip of disappointment from the guests at Jordan's sudden departure, the revelers had resumed enjoying the party. The fact that they'd all stayed into the wee hours of the night was a testament to the party's success and, thankfully, their lack of awareness of any underlying tension among the major players.

Dressed in her boxers and tee, Mac leaned back on the propped-up pillow of her bed, unable to sleep. Haley and Megan had insisted on coming in with her and she knew, from their reluctance to leave, that they were worried about her. She assured them she was exhausted and would go straight to sleep.

An hour later, sitting in bed wide awake, she knew her assurances had been a lie designed to allow her to be alone with her thoughts. Now those thoughts were proving to be poor bedfellows, and she wished she had a real person to talk to.

Her blinking laptop offered personal contact, but Mac shunned its false promises. Resigned to her insomnia, she reached for the book on her nightstand and lost herself in the fictional love lives of Shannon and Dylan.

> Dylan wasn't the type to wait for rejection. She knew, the moment Shannon clothed herself, that their romantic interlude was over and she'd been silly to hope she'd found someone to share the joys of life with, who was content with nothing more. She had no desire to reason or explain. It was time to move on.
>
> Why, then, was she feeling sudden resistance to her usual path away from the reaches of love and commitment? Shannon's profession of love had lit a fire inside her, but surely it was only the flame of lust she felt licking at her intransigence. Dodging the danger sure to encase her should she stay to find out, Dylan dressed quickly and left. Her departure was acknowledged by nothing more than a steely gaze.

Jordan was alone in the lobby. Despite her strong buzz, she knew where she was, but she didn't recall the trek downtown. She stared back through the glass doors and contemplated the starry night beyond. The revelations of the evening still swam in her head. She was angry and lonely, and she wasn't sure what to do about either emotion. During the past couple of hours at Fuse, she'd consumed one iced vodka after the next as if the act of drinking was her life's purpose. The rooftop patio had been buzzing with activity befitting a Friday night. Couples stargazed, singles mingled, and everyone was dressed to see and be seen. Normally, Jordan would have focused her attention on the many attractive women in attendance, but tonight her focus was inward. The presence of people was merely a buffer to the loneliness she felt within.

Pressing the button to Rebeca's loft, she waited for the occupant to respond.

"Yes?"

"It's Jordan. I'm downstairs. Buzz me up."

A click signaled the glass door to the elevators was open and Jordan pushed her way through. When she reached Rebeca's door, she paused. What the hell was she doing here? Ignoring the question, she rang the bell and hardly had time to draw a breath before she was staring at Rebeca. A short blue silk robe clung to every curve, leaving no doubt she had nothing on underneath. Yet she stood in the doorway as if fully dressed and ready for anything.

"Good evening, Dr. Wagner. I thought you might be making a house call."

Not the response Jordan had expected her visit to elicit. She'd worked up her anger on the way over, ready to unleash it on the woman who'd played her so masterfully. A little leg wasn't going to dissuade her from her original mission.

"What the fuck were you doing with Mackenzie?"

"Why, darling, are you jealous?" Rebeca batted her eyelashes.

"Jealous?"

"Oh, you are, aren't you?" Rebeca crooned. "I'm sorry, I didn't mean to make you jealous. You should know you're the one I want to be with."

Jordan was confused and wasn't sure whether to attribute it to the many drinks she'd had or whether Rebeca simply wasn't making sense. She stared at her, attempting to understand what was going on. Rebeca reached out and gently put one arm across Jordan's shoulders. As she did, her robe slipped slightly, revealing more than leg.

She whispered in Jordan's ear, "Let's take this inside. I don't want to share you with my neighbors."

Jordan, exhausted by the evening's events, allowed herself to be led into the living room. She sank down on the leather couch. Rebeca curled up next to her and began whispering enticements.

Jordan shed her fatigue and sprang from the couch. "We went out twice. Where do you get off thinking we have a relationship?" Increasing anger elevated the volume of her exclamations. "You said you weren't looking for a relationship. No strings attached. All play, no love."

Rebeca looked genuinely surprised at Jordan's anger. "I lied," she said simply. "Don't get me wrong, play is nice. But what kind of woman wants nothing more than to fuck around? You didn't mean all that crap in your profile, either, did you? I saw through your façade and I could tell you were trying to ward off all but the truly worthy. Right?"

"I'm not hearing this."

Rebeca didn't seem to notice Jordan's mumbled reply, intent as she was on pleading her case. "You needed a little encouragement to realize how you feel about me. When you stopped taking my calls, I decided to take matters into my own hands." With no sign of a response, Rebeca continued, "I figured all I had to do was make you jealous. What better way than to date someone close to you, so you'd see what you were missing?"

Jordan's anger was as much for herself as for the woman standing before her. "You think you are 'truly worthy,' huh? Well, I have news for you. If it's me you're holding out for, you're not worthy of much. Mackenzie is a better person than either you or I could ever dream of being. Anyone who hurts a friend of mine hurts me, and I'm not only an unworthy catch, I'm also a completely unforgiving bitch."

She paused to catch her breath while Rebeca looked at her like she was an alien who'd landed on planet Earth to spread tidings of ill will. Jordan decided it wasn't necessary to expound on the subject. Rebeca wasn't getting the message and she probably never would. Why, oh why, had she ever gone out with this crazy, manipulative she-devil? Walking toward the door, she refused to look back or respond to the spiteful epithets Rebeca hurled her way. She was thankful to reach the hall and escape the building without having a heavy object thrown at her.

Catching a cab in downtown Dallas was an iffy proposition at best. Jordan decided to make her way back to Fuse and let the valet attendant work his magic in exchange for a generous tip. As she walked, Rebeca's words echoed in her head: *What kind of woman wants nothing more than to fuck around? You didn't mean all that crap...* Putting aside the fact that Rebeca was a master manipulator, she turned the words over in her head, looking for signs of truth in the blunt proclamation. Had she really meant everything she'd written in the profile for Skin Deep? No strings, no love, no relationships? If so, the question about her worth was valid.

But she hadn't a clue as to the answer.

CHAPTER FOURTEEN

It feels weird having brunch without Jordan." Megan glanced around. Mac had been clear when they arrived. Jordan would not be joining them for brunch this Sunday morning. She had been purposely vague, though, about the reason for Jordan's absence.

"Mac's in the kitchen," Haley said. "You gals have a few minutes to gossip freely."

Aimee threw a breadstick across the table. "You, hush. We're not gossiping. We're merely worried about our friends. Does anyone have a clue about what happened the other night? I haven't been able to get a word out of Mac."

"Easy with the breadstick projectiles," Haley said. "I know you're both concerned, but Mac will share when she's ready. Obviously, whatever happened at Jordan's party set them both on edge."

"You're right, honey," Megan conceded. "It's hard not to wonder, though."

"Wonder what?"

The question wasn't Haley's, and Megan mentally berated herself for letting Mac sneak up on her. She decided she may as well plunge right in. "We were wondering what happened between you and Jordan."

Mac braced herself. She knew her friends had been waiting

for an explanation. She wasn't sure where to begin, nor was she sure she had the energy to tell the tale. She'd thought long and hard about the scene in her office the night of Jordan's party and had concluded that Rebeca had played them both. Still, she felt a lingering sense of doubt about Jordan's true feelings. Was she jealous that Mac could also attract beautiful women? She'd never felt Jordan was anything but supportive of her, but perhaps she'd taken too much for granted.

A breadstick-turned-wand captured her attention. "Hocus pocus, we need you to focus." Aimee, making use of the projectile from earlier, tried to rouse her from her spell.

"Jordan and I had a big fight. A bad one," Mac blurted out.

"We figured as much."

"Do you want to hear this or not?"

"Now you want to fight with us?" Aimee put a hand on Mac's shoulder and pulled her close. "I'm teasing. Sweetie, we're here for you. Tell us as much or as little as you want."

"I don't know where to start. Rebeca, the woman I met online and went out with a few times, showed up at the party. Well, she wasn't invited. As it turns out, Jordan had met her online too, and slept with her the first night they went out."

"Ouch." Aimee spoke for the group. "I'm guessing you found this out at the party?"

Mac nodded. "Sure did. In a crazy, jealous throw down. Jordan walked in when I was telling Rebeca I was irritated because she'd shown up uninvited. Jordan assumed I was trying to hide something and that I didn't want her to know I was dating Rebeca. Meanwhile, I had no idea the two of them had gone out before. There I was, introducing them to each other."

"What did Rebeca do while you two were fighting over her?"

"That's the weird thing. She flirted with both of us. And when I told her to get the hell out, she tried to get Jordan to leave with her."

"Weird is an understatement," Aimee said. "What did Jordan do?"

"She told Rebeca to get lost, and then she left. For all I know, they hooked up later."

"Do you think they did?" Megan looked dismayed.

"I don't know what to think. From the moment Jordan walked in my office, she was looking for a fight. I've seen her that angry before, but not at me. It was almost as if she was already worked up about something."

The moment the words left her lips, realization hit. What was it Grace had told her? Jordan had seen her father there with Grace. Mac could only guess what she'd witnessed to stoke such fury.

"Mac, what is it?" Megan prompted.

Mac hesitated. She was sure she was the only one at the table privy to the details of Jordan's history with the other Dr. Wagner. Though Jordan hadn't asked her to keep her estrangement from her father a secret, she'd never shared this part of Jordan's life with the rest of the group. Frankly, there had never been a reason to discuss it. But she sensed more was going on with her right now than the fight about Rebeca, and she wasn't in a position to offer solace. She was still stinging from Jordan's angry words, and she doubted Jordan wanted to be around her anyway.

"I think I know why Jordan was so upset by the time she found Rebeca in my office," Mac said, deciding she wouldn't wait till Jordan found out her confidences had been revealed. Instead she would tell her as soon as she could.

She went on to share with their friends the details about how Jordan's mother had died and the alienation between father and daughter. She didn't have to explain why Jordan had overreacted to the budding relationship between her estranged father and Grace, a woman she loved and respected like a mother. Relaying the tale, Mac felt a stab of pain for the hurt and betrayal Jordan must be feeling. As mad as she was at the way Jordan had left things hanging between them, she resolved to reach out to her grieving friend.

❖

"You are unbelievable." Grace towered over Jordan's desk and made no attempt to lower her voice in deference to the obviously pounding head resting there. "Your eyes are bloodshot and you need to change your clothes."

Jordan gingerly stared up at her. She could only manage a few words. "Leave me alone."

Meant to be an order, it came out like a plea. She craved comfort, but Grace was one of the people she had no desire to see, hear, or talk to right now. Feeling intensely sorry for herself, she let her head fall back on the desk. In addition to self-pity, she was feeling the effects the last week's activities. She'd been out every night since her birthday, but celebration had been the last thing on her mind. Self-flagellation was more like it, and the combination of too much alcohol and no sleep was beginning to take its toll. Today had been especially long and overbooked.

"Get up, Jordan. I mean it. You're not going to sit here and sulk all day. It's your choice if you want to stay out all night, every night, doing who knows what. But you also have an obligation to your business and the patients that rely on you."

Unable to ignore Grace's persistent presence, Jordan raised her head. "Oh yeah? Well, bullshit. My patients only rely on me to reinforce their vanity, definitely not a life-saving skill. Let them figure out how to save their own self-images."

"Fine, Jordan. I'll tell them their doctor is too hungover and self-involved to be of any assistance to them."

Grace's words pierced, and a combination of anger and hurt propelled Jordan to her feet. "What the hell do you care? You've pretended to be a mother figure to me all these years and it turns out you were trying to take her place all along. Why should I listen to your lectures on how not to hurt other people's feelings? Why don't you get out? We both know you'd rather be with *him* anyway."

Grace steeled her expression, willing herself not to burst into tears. Jordan was indeed like a daughter to her, though because of their roles, she'd never had to play the heavy. She struggled with competing compulsions. The desire to be a strong role model beat out her usual stance as the loving, but permissive older friend.

"I've never wanted to replace your mother's memory," she said gently. "It's true, I do love you as if you were my own, but if I'd ever wanted to be like a real mother to you, I would have told you long time ago what a stubborn, thick-headed young woman you are. Especially when it comes to how you treat your father."

"My father is a shallow man with no feelings," Jordan spat back. "He didn't shed one tear when my mother died."

"Just because you didn't see him express his emotions doesn't mean he didn't have any. Maybe he wasn't willing to burden you with his grief. Your father loved your mother as much as any person has loved another."

"Bullshit. If he loved her, he should have done something to stop her from dying." Jordan paused, but decided not to let what she knew to be irrational thoughts stop her rant. "All he's ever cared about is making money off other people's vanity, and now look at me. I'm exactly like him. I hate him and I hate myself."

Grace moved quickly around the desk and encircled Jordan with her arms. Holding Jordan's head against her shoulder, she rocked her gently. "Honey, relax and breathe. You and your father are good people, though you are so much alike, loving the two of you is destined to drive me to distraction. I need to tell you something. Something important, but I don't want you to misunderstand my motives."

Jordan sniffed. "What?"

"I loved your mother very much. She was a good friend to me. And like a good friend, she trusted me with a secret, something only she and your father knew about."

"Dammit, Grace. Quit being cagey. Spit it out."

"Shush. It's not that easy. Do you remember Michael Forte? The doctor your father practiced with when you were much younger?"

"Yes, I remember him. Michael and Dad went to school together. They were best friends."

"Well, I could sugarcoat what I have to say, but I won't. Your mother had an affair with Michael. Your father knew, but he never let on. She knew he knew. She even tried to talk to him about it, but he wouldn't discuss it. They never had a chance to work things out. Her cancer appeared so suddenly, and with such force, that they spent all their time on last-ditch efforts to save her life, and then preparing for the inevitable. But he never stopped loving her and he never told a soul."

"Then how do you know he even knew?"

"Your mother told me the whole tale a couple of days before she died. She asked me to keep it a secret. She didn't want her one big mistake to color your memory of her. But she also wanted me to make sure you always knew how much your father loves you. The way I see it, her last wishes are in conflict, and I have to break one promise to keep the other."

Paralyzed by a swirl of emotions, Jordan stared at the woman who'd been her most important role model all her adult life. Anger and confusion about Grace's relationship with her father trumped the feelings about her mother's deathbed confession. "Why the hell are you telling me this now?"

"Because I know your mother was scared you two would grow apart without her around to bridge the differences between you. I know she would hate what's happened." Grace paused. "Jordan, you're exactly like him. You act like you don't feel anything to make people think they can't get to you."

"Are you dating my father?" Jordan shouted the question.

"I love your father, but our relationship is complicated."

"My question is simple. Let me ask it another way. How long after my mother died did you two wait before you decided you couldn't stand it anymore?"

"Jordan, don't say these things. You'll regret them later."

"Fine, don't answer. I didn't expect you to." Jordan moved out of Grace's reach and stalked to the door. "Cancel my appointments for the rest of the week." She had a vague recollection this was a week she'd planned to take off anyhow, to have some time out around her birthday. "There shouldn't be much to cancel. I'll get Dr. Smith to cover rounds and any emergencies. Use the service to get hold of me, only if it's absolutely necessary."

"Are you two ready to tell me what you want your new house to look like?"

Megan turned toward the voice and blurted, "Haley thinks Jordan's in love with Mackenzie."

Haley nearly jumped out of her chair. "All I said was I have a hunch about those two. I don't have anything concrete to base it on."

Aimee laughed as she closed the office door behind her. "And here I was, prepared to help you find your dream home, and you're sitting in here concocting wild tales. Near as I can tell, Jordan's never been in love with anyone, let alone her best friend who she isn't speaking to. Haley, what have you been drinking?"

"Forget I said anything. I withdraw my wild tale. Let's talk houses." Haley leaned toward Aimee's desk and imitated a prospective buyer.

Megan poked her in the side. "Oh no, you don't." She knew Haley well enough to know that she chose to share her thoughts only after they were fully formed. "You know something. Tell us."

"I don't *know* anything. I think Jordan has feelings for Mackenzie beyond mere friendship. I think she's scared of those feelings because she's never felt them before for anyone, let alone for her best friend."

Megan's mind was racing and finally crossed the finish line. "She told you the night you had dinner, right?"

"She didn't say anything specifically, but she asked a lot of questions about love and commitment interspersed with possessive comments about Mac. I drew my own conclusions."

"Wow." Aimee could only muster up the one word.

Megan spoke next. "Do you think Mac has a clue?"

Aimee regained her ability to speak. "I would venture to say she has no idea. They've been friends forever. I'm sure Mac never imagined their friendship being anything more.

At least not in the time I've known her. She and Jordan were friends long before I met them."

"Lovers often evolve into friends, why is the reverse not possible?" Megan posed. "I think they'd make a great couple. They have a lot of the same interests, but their temperaments are unique enough to give them good balance."

"A nice way of saying they're so different they'll probably fight all the time," Aimee observed wryly.

"They hardly ever fight, except for this latest."

"Nothing like love to heat things up a bit." Aimee frowned. "To tell the truth, I had a similar thought about Jordan a couple of weeks ago, but I decided I must be losing my mind. Now I'm thinking maybe my gut was right at the time."

Megan turned to her wife. "Haley, you've been awfully quiet. What's on your mind?"

"Oh, I was calculating how long it'll take before one of you calls one of them to break the good news. Maybe you'll split the task? You could call Jordan, and Aimee could call Mac."

Megan recognized the gentle humor beneath what appeared to be sarcasm. Her wife's skill was in fixing physical problems. Working in emergency medicine, she didn't delve below what she could see in the short period of time she spent with each patient. Megan, on the other hand, spent hours delving into her patients' minds. Haley had expressed, on more than one occasion, admiration for what she viewed as the more grueling job, and she understood that Megan had difficulty turning off her analytical mind.

"Very funny." Megan was already formulating a plan. "Actually, my love, I was thinking you and I could swing by Jordan's office on the way home."

"Yeah, well, I'll wait in the car."

CHAPTER FIFTEEN

Jordan hit the Austin city limit at the tail end of rush-hour traffic. Things had changed a lot since she had been a young student at UT. More houses, more big-box stores, more malls, more roads, more people. Proof positive change is not always for the better.

She drove until she could cut off the highway, then took a jagged shortcut through downtown. The sun still lit up the sky, but the Congress Street Bridge was already lined with spectators jockeying for the best spots to view the seasonal flight of the bats at dusk. Austin was home to the largest urban bat colony in North America. From March to November, about a million and a half Mexican free-tail bats flew out from under the bridge each night in search of an insect dinner. With fondness, she recalled taking several dates to see the spectacular sight. For women not native to Austin, the nightly flight of the bats was a thrilling event, perfect for a student's budget.

Things were different now, Jordan reflected as she turned into the drive of the Four Seasons on San Jacinto. Tossing her keys to the valet, she strode into the lobby, waving off the bellman coming her way. She didn't have any luggage, having left her office with no destination in mind, and in her tailored suit and heels, and she felt way too Dallas-looking for this laid-back city. Producing her platinum Amex, she requested a large, private suite with a view of Town Lake. Within moments she would be able to watch the bats from her very own balcony.

As soon as she had her swipe-card, Jordan took the elevator to her room. She'd no sooner switched on the light and strode to the balcony when dusk swept the evening sky. The throng of bats left their daybeds underneath the Congress Street Bridge and took to the sky as one big banner of blackness. Standing in solitude on the balcony, Jordan felt the darkness seep inside her. The crowds of people gathered on the banks of the lake and those watching from charter boats on the water, all enjoying the camaraderie of this event, seemed to mock her solitude, and she was struck by a pervasive sense of loneliness.

Unable to stand the sight, she picked up the phone to order a bottle of Scotch and a light meal as an excuse to wash it down, then asked to be connected to the concierge. She needed jeans, loafers, casual shirts to keep from sticking out like a sore thumb, but there was no way she was going back out into the horrendous traffic to purchase clothes for her stay. The eager concierge took down her sizes and favorite brands and guaranteed to have several outfits delivered shortly.

Jordan leaned against the headboard, and moments later the exhaustion of too many feelings washed away her resistance to sleep.

Stress and lack of sleep combined to make Mac feel like skipping her morning ride. A glance out the window reinforced her desire to crawl back under the covers. The sky was gray and clouds hung low, and it wasn't as if Jordan was suddenly going to appear and join her. She'd left messages all week, but

Jordan hadn't returned a single call. Pulling her book from the nightstand, Mac promised herself she would only read a few pages and then she'd face the world.

Shannon hadn't called. It seemed futile to reach out to her now. Dylan had hoped against hope her new lover would see her way clear to the inevitable truth. They were better off without strings, without commitment. She had tested the other way. The way of pledges and promises of forever. That way had proved treacherous and tricky, undeserving of her trust. Shannon still believed in promises and had decided to seek those promises from someone else. She would learn, on her own, that forever was a fickle thing. Dylan could only hope she wouldn't suffer too much on her journey.

Perhaps, she thought, Shannon would return to her one day, as resolved as Dylan was to live without the burden of promises no one intends to keep.

Mac couldn't bring herself to read another depressing word. She shut her book, tore herself from the comfort of the covers, dressed in cycling shorts and a jersey, and made the short drive to the Lakeside.

At this hour, Sally and Nick were the only ones present. Mac made herself a cup of coffee and a protein shake, and escaped before conversation could turn to the events of the week before and why her best friend had dropped off the face of the earth. Mac hadn't been herself since the party, and she knew her friends were worried, but she couldn't muster the energy to put them at ease about her state of mind. It had been all she could do to make it to work each day.

With the excuse that she wanted to get her ride in before

the heat of the day became unbearable, she ducked interaction, grabbed her mighty Isis road bike, and headed quickly for the trail. Resolving to take a long ride to clear her head, she eased into a steady pace as she cycled to the east, past sailboats tethered to the docks waiting for the right winds to coax their captains into sailing the day away.

So, Jordan had left town. Mac tried to make excuses for her, knowing the discovery about Grace and Dr. Wagner senior must have caught her completely off guard. And she had no idea what the whole Rebeca fiasco had been about. Mac felt someone was being manipulated, but she wasn't sure who or why. In any event, the debacle had been enough to make Mac suspend her profile from all interested viewers. She'd officially put the kibosh on her online dating adventures.

As she passed by the Arboretum, she realized she'd already gone through the one water bottle she'd hastily grabbed from the restaurant, and she decided to make a pit stop at the 7-Eleven near the Gaston Street Bridge. Leaning her bike against the store's front window, she unzipped her seat bag and extracted the tiny wallet she kept stowed with her bike gear. The wallet contained a copy of her driver's license, a twenty dollar bill, her insurance card, and two emergency phone numbers. The first of those was Dr. Jordan Wagner's. Seeing the card, Mac paused. She wasn't even sure Jordan would come running if she had an emergency. Pushing the thought away, she quickly ducked inside the store. She didn't bother chaining her bike. So many cyclists made this place a regular stop on their route, they always watched out for each other's rides.

A light rain started to fall as she downed a Gatorade several minutes later. Mac clipped back into her pedals, enjoying the slight relief the scattered drops provided against the heat of the day. The road provided steeper hills than the path along the lake, but Mac was in the mood for strenuous exercise so she chose the tough route. The pain she felt in her muscles blocked some of the pain in her heart and mind. She'd had two dates as a result of her online match making venture. The first had been a non-event. Charla wasn't her type, but at least the experience of dating her hadn't been traumatic. The same couldn't be said of Rebeca Blixen.

Mac didn't have a clue what had happened there. Maybe Jordan was full of crap when she said her fling with Rebeca was all about sex. Maybe she had feelings for her. Maybe finding her with Mac on the heels of the revelation about her father and Grace had sent her into a tailspin. *What kind of friend am I,* Mac thought, *letting my feelings get in the way?* She should have been supportive of her best friend, right when she was needed most. Mac yearned to set things straight between them. If only Jordan would return her calls.

Aggravated, she turned her focus back to her exercise and challenged herself to race up the next hill. The gradient was steep and Mac started downshifting early in the climb to ease the effect of the ascent on her legs. She nodded at a fellow rider as she whooshed by, feeling the change in pace behind her as the rider pedaled faster to catch up. Nothing motivated a cyclist like being passed on the trail. Mac was a smart rider and had lots of experience taking big hills. In the years she and Jordan had cycled together, they'd done many organized rides all over the state and were used to all kinds of terrain. She knew to start working her gears before climbing to minimize the effect on both her body and bike. Trying to shift into the easier gears midway up a steep incline would throw a bike chain.

Mac saw the shadow of the approaching rider as he pulled up alongside. He was pedaling hard and huffing at the strain of the climb. Dropping back, she decided to let him pass her by and keep his ego intact. As he strained to pull in front of her, she glanced down at her bike's computer and checked her cadence. In that split second a chaotic sequence of events begin to unfold.

As his bike chain dropped, the cyclist in front of her went quickly from trying to be first up the hill to trying to keep his balance. In an attempt to regain control, he stood up on both pedals, but his action had exactly the opposite effect. With his weight removed from the seat of the bike, his tires lost all traction on the slick pavement and his rear wheel jerked wildly to the left. Losing control, he frantically tried to clip out of his pedals.

Mac's experience riding in wet conditions told her disaster was imminent. She swerved to avoid the bike careening into her path, but she wasn't fast enough to avoid the collision. The impact sent her spinning in the opposite direction, still clipped to her own falling bike, and careening straight into the path of an oncoming car. The driver had no time to react and his swerve didn't come in time. The impact separated Mac from her bike, and they both bounced off the hood before landing back on the road.

Chapter Sixteen

"Grace, the hospital is on line one, looking for Dr. Wagner."

Grace looked up from the mound of paperwork occupying her attention and grimaced at the practice's receptionist. "I thought I told you Dr. Wagner is not available for the rest of the week. If it's an emergency, tell them to page Dr. Smith."

"I told them already, but they insist they need to talk to Dr. Wagner."

Grace grabbed the receiver from the handset on her desk and stabbed at the flashing button. This was the third time the hospital had called for Jordan, despite having been told she was not available. "Who am I speaking to?" Grace demanded.

A young male gave his name and repeated a request to speak with Dr. Wagner.

"As our receptionist told you a moment ago, Dr. Wagner is not available," Grace said sharply. "I would be happy to provide you with the pager number for Dr. Smith. He's handling her cases in her absence." She paused to give the persistent caller time to prepare to take down the number, but he wasn't finished.

"It's very important that I speak with her in person."

Grace wasn't about to admit that she couldn't call Jordan

even if she wanted to, since she didn't know her whereabouts and all she would get was her voicemail. "No, I am not going to disturb her without good reason. Dr. Smith is handling her calls and I would appreciate it if you would respect the arrangement."

There was a long silence. The clerk apparently decided to take a different approach and let loose with a little more information. "Dr. Wagner is listed as a personal emergency contact for a Ms. Lewis. That's the reason I need to speak to her."

"You mean Mackenzie Lewis?" Grace's pulse shot up, and as she listened, her frustration quickly changed to anxiety. "Oh my, I'm sorry I was so short with you. I'll find Dr. Wagner right away."

After hanging up the phone, Grace collected herself for a few seconds, then punched an open line and dialed another number, waiting impatiently through the rings.

"Jacob, I need you. Now!"

Brunch on the private terrace was relaxing. If she'd planned this right, she could have taken a regular vacation and enjoyed the amenities a whole lot longer. Pouring herself some more coffee and juice, Jordan wondered how long it would be before she got bored with her own company. Well, there were plenty of women in Austin. Some of them might enjoy an evening with a successful surgeon in a four-star hotel. Even as the thought formed, Jordan doubted her own proclamation. Resolving to at least try to enjoy her own company, she took her coffee and her copy of the *Austin American-Statesman*, and stretched out on the padded lounge chair.

The news of the day went unnoticed as she reflected on the

events that had driven her out of Dallas. She'd never thought of Grace entirely as a mother substitute, but apparently her father had made the transition to replace his wife with the closest remaining strong female presence when she died. Frankly, Jordan had mixed feelings about the idea of an intimate relationship between Grace and her father. Though she didn't mind having Grace as part of the family, she wasn't altogether certain she wanted the additional closeness with her father that his relationship with Grace would bring. She and her father hadn't actually been a family since her mother's death. They'd each gone off in solitude, and the hurt they carried became a weighty distance between them. Neither knew, anymore, how to bridge the gap formed by grief, and they had both come to accept the separation with ambivalence.

For the first time since her mother's death, Jordan tried to embrace how her father felt. He must have been devastated when he learned about the affair. She recalled night after night when he'd stayed by her mom's side in the hospital and then at home, where hospice care workers tried to ease her suffering. He didn't eat, sleep, or work, apparently viewing all such tasks as distractions designed to divert the healing power mere presence might provide. During that time, he'd been absent to Jordan, barely seeming to notice her existence. Her memory, previously clouded by her personal grief, was clearer now. Her father had been a man obsessed, and his singular focus was powerless against the cancer that consumed the woman he loved unconditionally.

Could she ever love a woman the way he loved her mother? Pained by the events of the last week, Jordan closed her eyes and left the thought unanswered. She wasn't sure how much time had drifted by when she felt a presence in the room and jerked awake. Glancing back through the patio doors, she saw

CARSEN TAITE

a form moving. Still drowsy from her nap, she slowly opened the patio door and poked her head inside, startling the maid.

"Oh, miss. I didn't see you. Would you like me to come back later?"

Jordan smiled. "No need. Go ahead and finish."

As the maid gathered and replaced the towels in the room, Jordan picked up her BlackBerry, which was rattling on the nightstand. She didn't recognize the number flashing on the screen and let the call go to voicemail, joining ten other missed calls on the device. She pondered her options, trying to decide whether she was ready to start picking up her messages and easing herself back into everyday life again. Maybe not. She called the front desk.

"Dr. Wagner, what a coincidence, I was about to ring your room."

Momentarily confused at the greeting, Jordan said, "I want to stay for a few extra days, is this room available?"

"I would be happy to check for you, Dr. Wagner. In the meantime, your service called and asked me to get a message to you right away."

"What's the message?"

"They want you to call the emergency room at Presbyterian Hospital immediately. Ask for Dr. Tyler."

"Thanks." Jordan kept her annoyance to herself. She'd expected Grace to field her calls and make the necessary arrangements. "And there's no problem with you keeping the room you're in. Thank you for choosing the Four Seasons."

Jordan ended the call and immediately dialed her paging service. As she waited for the operator to pick up the line, she examined the list of missed calls on her BlackBerry. Her paging service, the office, Aimee, Megan, Marty, Grace's cell phone. A sense of dread enveloped her and she hung up, immediately redialing Presbyterian Hospital. She shouted her request to

• 164 •

the operator. The line rang a thousand times, her grip on the handset tightening with each passing moment.

"Emergency room," a harried voice announced.

"Dr. Jordan Wagner. Dr. Tyler paged me."

"Ah, Dr. Wagner. You're listed as an emergency contact for one of our patients. Dr. Tyler's with her right now, but I'll let her know you called and she'll call you right back. What's the best number for you?"

Jordan knew of only one person who listed her as an emergency contact, the same person she listed whenever she was required to provide such information. Her stomach clenched and she felt the handset shake as the realization swept through her. Mac was in trouble and she was two hundred miles away. Jordan grasped at the tiniest strand of hope. "Tell me the name of the patient."

Until she heard the name out loud, she didn't have to feel the full force of pain in knowing her best friend needed her and she was in no position to help.

"I'm not able to give out personal information. Dr. Tyler will call you in a couple of minutes."

"Need I remind you, you called me? This is ridiculous. Tell me the name." A command this time, delivered in the demanding tone of a surgeon. Jordan waited for compliance.

The hospital worker on the other end responded to her confident demand the way most people did. He resolved to spare himself a problem. "The patient's name is Mackenzie Lewis."

Jordan sighed, any last hope deflated at the news. She quickly rattled off her cell phone number for the call back and disconnected the line. She grabbed her purse and ran to the elevator, willing everything to move faster to accommodate her frantic mood. A couple of guests were hovering indecisively at the concierge's desk, perusing day trip brochures.

Jordan crowded them until they stepped back. "I need a charter plane to get me to Dallas immediately."

Mac stirred. The tiny movement sent waves of pain through her body, blocking her ability to figure out where she was. Through the slits of her barely opened eyes, she saw a shadowy curtain surrounding her. She realized she was in a bed, but not her own. She peered around, careful to let her eyes move without assistance from her head, which was a pounding source of pain. Her left arm was in a sling and the slightest movement was pure anguish. The core of her body was encased in a bandage and she sensed she shouldn't try to move.

Her eyes failed to find the source of the voice she'd heard mere seconds ago. Her memory of the words was vague, but the tone was comforting and she longed to see the speaker. But no one was in the room. Weary from the effort of her visual search, Mac closed her eyes and let herself slide into the fog of her thoughts.

CHAPTER SEVENTEEN

E xcuse me, ma'am. You can't go in there."
Jordan didn't miss a step in her stride, but she did glance back at the nurse trailing after her. "Oh yeah, well, stop me."

She burst through the double doors leading to the hospital's recovery room. She didn't have any current information about Mac's status, knowing only no news at this point was good news. The flight had seemed interminably long as she waited out the minutes for a call from one of the doctors attending to Mac. Not hearing from them meant no life-or-death decisions were necessary, which was certainly a relief, but the communications void had made her crazy with worry.

As the plane landed, she received a call from a nurse stating only that Mac was stable and in recovery. Jordan paid an outrageous amount to get a cab driver to race the several miles from Love Field to Presbyterian Hospital. She ignored the nurse who continued to follow her, warning that she was going to notify security. As she entered the recovery room, Jordan stalked past beds separated only by filmy curtains suspended from the ceiling. Glancing at the charts hanging at the end of the occupied beds, she quickly ascertained where her best friend lay.

Pulling back the curtain, she gasped. Mac was lying on her back, her eyes closed. She was pale and drawn. Small splotches of blood were crusted on her face and she looked like a battle victim. Her left arm was in a sling. Jordan sank into the chair beside her bed and wept. "Oh Mac, I don't know what I would do if I lost you. I love you."

Her confession was met with a slight stir from the bed's occupant, but Mac's eyes didn't open. Jordan slipped one of her hands over Mac's and rested her head against the mattress, overwhelmed by the events of the day. As she shook off the fatigue, she felt a touch from behind and glanced over her shoulder into the eyes of her father.

Too tired to maintain her usual irritation at this man she had grown so far apart from, she asked, "What are you doing here?" Her words reflected a genuine surprise to see him in this place, at this time.

"I've been here for hours. I came as soon as I heard."

"You heard?" Jordan could hear her own dull confusion.

"Grace called me when she couldn't reach you. We were worried sick about Mackenzie. Despite the fact I haven't seen her in years, there was a time I thought of her like a daughter. And I know how important she is to you. I know Dr. Tyler. She's a fine doctor and, as a family courtesy, she let me assist so I could be close by."

Jordan ignored all the other questions rising to her mind at the moment and posed one. "How is she?"

"She's going to be fine. She took a pretty good hit from an SUV, but from what I hear her bike took the brunt of the impact. She has a dislocated left collarbone and a couple of broken ribs. The scrapes on her face are slight. She didn't need my services at all."

Jordan pointed at the chest tube. "Pneumothorax?"

Her father nodded. "One of the fractured ribs punctured

her left lung, causing collapse. The tube should be able to come out in a few days."

"Thank you for being here."

"You *should* thank me for being here. One of the nurses was racing down the hall with security in tow. I think they were preparing to forcibly remove you from the hospital. I explained to them that the wild-looking woman they were pursuing is actually one of Dallas's finest surgeons and persuaded them to back off."

Jordan glanced down, seeing for the first time what the hospital personnel had observed when she arrived. She was wrinkled and scruffy from the hasty flight, and she bet her hair looked like a bird nest. Actually, her father didn't look much better. He wore blue scrubs, and tufts of usually well-coiffed dark brown hair jutted out in a variety of directions. Despite the lapse in grooming, Jordan observed that neither age nor personal misfortune had slowed him down. He was the pinnacle of deluxe plastic surgery success in Dallas. Since Dallas had no shortage of plastic surgeons vying for the ever-growing market, being on top was quite an achievement. Her father operated a thriving practice in the heart of the Park Cities, with a six-month waiting list of wealthy patients and countless associates willing to work like first-year residents, their eyes gleaming with expectations of their own future fortunes.

Her goal was to top her father's success with her own achievement. Her plans included expansion of her facility to rival the accommodations of a five-star spa resort. No medicinal clinic atmosphere for her wealthy, accustomed-to-being-pampered clientele. Taking a page from the many luxury spas that dotted the city, Jordan planned discreet, deluxe accommodations to provide the perfect setting for her clients to hide away from the pressures of the outside world while enjoying the rejuvenating experience of a surgical makeover.

Four years into private practice, she was well on her way to taking her place among Dallas's elite. She'd spent the time working her ass off, using every means at her disposal to make sure her name was synonymous with success in her field. Though fortunate enough to have a solid source of financial resources when she graduated her fellowship, she didn't rely on her inherited wealth. Instead she approached business development with the same razor-sharp precision she brought to the surgical suite. Jordan sought privileges at all the local hospitals, taking the associated requirement of nights on call in stride. Every busy night on call generated more patients filling her office for follow-ups in the weeks after. When she wasn't on call, she was marketing her business, using her best public relations tool: herself. Magnetic and personable, when she appeared at networking functions people were drawn to the charming surgeon. She made it a point to be active in several local business organizations, including the local GLBT Chamber of Commerce. All of these efforts focused on a singular objective: to be the most successful plastic surgeon in Dallas, bar none. To exceed her father's accomplishments and expectations.

Now, standing in front of him, looking into chocolate brown eyes surrounded by red streaks and framed by dark circles and puffy skin, she realized he was only human. His normally clean-shaven face was eclipsed in shadow. Despite his disheveled appearance, he was smiling at her, though tentatively. Relieved to hear Mac was going to be okay, she couldn't help but return his cautious smile.

Perhaps encouraged by her response, he laid his hand on her shoulder and said, "Jordan, I love you. When you're ready, I need to talk to you about some things."

She never thought she'd hear herself saying the words, but they fell from her lips. "I think it's time."

His hand tightened. "I want us to heal the hurt between us. You're all the family I have and I don't want to lose you any more than I already have. When Grace called and told me to get to the hospital right away, the first thought I had was about you. I couldn't bear it if something happened to you, especially when we've been odds all this time. Seeing Mackenzie hurt like this made me realize time is precious. At any moment, life could be ripped away from us and I could lose the chance to show you exactly how much you mean to me."

Jordan's first response was wonder. Her father had just said more in a few seconds than she'd heard in years. Despite the armor she had in place, her resistance melted away, warmed by his declarations. In that moment, she realized she loved him and missed his presence in her life and, apparently, he loved and missed her too. Resolving to explore these feelings, she replied, "I love you too, Dad. We have a lot of repair work ahead. I'm willing to work on us if you are."

His answer was a hug, at first tentative, then strong and confident.

"Well, I never…"

Father and daughter, still embracing, turned as one toward the voice.

"As glad as I am to see you both getting along so well, I've come to throw you out." Grace's pronouncement was laced with a smile. "The recovery room nurse has prevailed upon me to convince my 'friends' to return to the waiting room. Come on, you two. Let's go."

Jordan stood her ground. "I'm not leaving her."

"Honey, she's going to be fine. She needs her rest. Besides, all your friends are waiting outside. You haven't talked to any of them yet, right?"

"They're here?" Was she the last to know about the accident?

Grace smiled. "Yes, and I'm sure they'd like to hear how Mackenzie's doing. She'll be in a room in a few hours and you can visit with her then."

Jordan wavered, knowing Grace was right. But she had some unfinished business and she wasn't going to leave the room until she took care of it. "I promise I'll be right out. You can tell Nurse Ratched, I'll only be five minutes. Let the gang know I'm on my way."

"You have five minutes." Grace took Jacob's arm and propelled him toward the door, telling Jordan, "See you in the waiting room."

Jordan sat back down in the chair by Mac's bed. Grasping Mac's hand with both of her own, she spoke from her heart. "There's never been anyone as special to me as you. You've always loved me, even when I have been decidedly unlovable. I know I've been a real jerk lately. Well, not lately. All the years I've known you, I never let myself admit I'm hopelessly in love with you. I've never been serious about anyone, because that would have been a betrayal of the feelings I have for you. No one else was ever good enough for you, as far as I was concerned, because they weren't me. They didn't know you, care about you, love you the way I do. While I set out to keep you from finding happiness with anyone else, I let my fear of commitment get in the way of telling you the truth. I want to spend the rest of my life showing you how much I love you. I hope it's not too late. I hope this knock on the head didn't cure you of all your romantic notions. Mackenzie Lewis, you're going to get better soon. And when you do, I am going to sweep you off your feet."

With her vow complete, Jordan kissed Mac lightly on the forehead and quietly slipped from the room.

❖

"Is she going to be okay?" several people asked at once.

"Yes. She's got a dislocated collarbone, a few broken ribs, and a bunch of scrapes and bruises. There's a chest tube pumping air into her lung until it heals on its own. It will take some time, but she's going to be fine." Jordan sank into one of the stiff waiting room chairs and signaled everyone else to take their seats as well. She was happy to be surrounded by her friends, but overwhelmed by the rapid-fire questions. The adrenaline rush of the trip from Austin was wearing off and the strain of worry was starting to take its toll.

"Where have you been?" Megan asked.

"I was in Austin. I came as soon as I heard." Before she could be subjected to an inquisition about her disappearance, she asked, "Where's the Lewis clan?"

"They're all here," Aimee said. "We got the report from the surgeon about twenty minutes ago, and then we sent them downstairs to get something to eat. The kids were going haywire and the doc said they wouldn't be able to see Mac for a few hours anyway."

"So, basically, I didn't tell you anything you didn't already know?"

Megan chimed in. "Grace said you were here, so we waited. I don't know how you got past us. Anyway, we wanted to get the skinny firsthand from the doctor we know and love. Besides, we've been worried about you."

Jordan blushed as Megan hugged her tight. Pulling back after the embrace, she surveyed the group. "It's good to see you all. I know I've been distant lately, but I swear everything's either okay or going to be okay soon. I promise."

"Let's go join the rest of the group for lunch," Haley suggested. "I bet they'll be glad to see the prodigal sister. Jeremy's been asking about you ever since they got here. He was completely unimpressed to be in the presence of a member of the Dallas Fire Department."

Jordan grinned at the slight to Haley's ego, knowing it was all for show. "Relax, stud. All you have to do is break out the hat and siren and I won't stand a chance." She ran a hand through her tangled hair. "If you all can stand to be seen with me looking like this, I could use something to eat. What do you say we find the inquiring young Jeremy and give him another report on his aunt Mac?"

The group hauled her to her feet and proudly escorted her to the fine dining establishment known as the hospital cafeteria.

CHAPTER EIGHTEEN

Mac wrinkled her nose at the wheelchair. "I hate to be the stereotypical stubborn patient, but I'd rather walk out of here on my own. After two days in this bed, I'm ready to be back on my feet."

"Banish those butch thoughts." Jordan pushed the chair closer to the bed. "The faster you get in the chair, the faster you get to blow this joint." Seeing the look of dismay on Mac's face, she continued, "Seriously, it could take weeks for your ribs to completely heal. Everything you do to minimize physical stress will help them heal faster."

"She's right." Haley added her two cents. "You need to take it easy for a while."

"What is this? Medical professionals gang up on poor patient day? Megan, you want to get in on this?"

"Not me. This doc prefers to focus on your mind." Megan leaned in and whispered, "But I promise you'll feel a lot better if you listen to these two so you can get the hell out of here."

"Fine, fine. Aimee, do you mind grabbing my bag?"

"Don't worry about a thing, missy. We'll pack up all this stuff and get it to your house. You could open your own florist shop." Aimee gestured toward the many colorful flower arrangements lining every surface. She directed her next question to Jordan. "Are you taking her straight home?"

Mac interrupted as Jordan started to answer. "She is not. We have a very necessary stop to make on the way."

"You are not going to work," Aimee said. "Sally and Nick have everything under control and you're under doctor's orders not to overexert yourself."

"Jeez, lighten up. I'm having a terrible shaved ice craving. There's nothing like being stuck in a hospital to make your cravings get out of control. I swear, I have to have one. We'll probably beat you to the house anyway."

"All right, addict. Enjoy your fix. We'll see you at the house."

Jordan couldn't help but notice how painful the ride was for her friend. Her M5 had arrived from Austin yesterday and she insisted on being the one to drive Mac home from the hospital. Over the last few days, she found she couldn't stand to be away from her and she was glad she had already planned to take the time off work so she didn't have to cancel all of her appointments. Yet even after spending days by Mac's side, she hadn't been able to wrap her mind around a way to bring them as close as she wanted them to be emotionally. Her head was filled with dreams, and in each one she and Mac were a happy couple. The problem was, she didn't know how to make the dreams a reality. The words had been so easy to speak aloud when Mac was unable to hear them. Now she had Mac's full attention, and words failed her.

"Penny for your thoughts?"

Startled, Jordan quickly recovered, trying for a jocular response. "They may not be worth a penny to you."

"That's kind of a funny thing to say. What do you mean?"

"Nothing. I was thinking you must have a lot on your mind without taking on my mental baggage."

Mac sighed. "My brain is doing aerobics right now. How will I work? How will I shower? The list is endless."

"Nick and Sally will take care of the restaurant. They both know how important it is to you that things keep running smoothly." Jordan paused to consider the decision she was about to announce. "Oh, and I'm moving in with you."

"You think so, huh?"

"Look, before you get started on how independent you are, hear me out. You need to take it easy for the next several weeks, which means some restrictions. No heavy lifting—even bending over could cause a lot of pain. And, you're going to have a hard time using your left arm for a while. The first time you need to tie your shoes, you're going to be glad I'm there. I have a lot of flexibility in my schedule and I know all your favorite foods, so who better to be your maid?"

"I'll think about it. In the meantime, I need a raspberry shaved ice with cream. On the double."

"Yes, ma'am."

Hours later, Mac was too tired to protest when Jordan made herself a bed in the spare room. Friends and family had spent the afternoon into evening celebrating her release from the hospital, and Jordan had fussed like a little old woman at the lateness of the hour before shoving everyone out. Secretly, Mac was glad Jordan was staying. Getting ready for bed had been a monumental task, and if Jordan hadn't been there she would probably have collapsed on top of the covers, fully dressed.

She knew her brothers were happy Jordan was sticking

around. Marty and Alice had initially insisted Mac stay with them during her recovery, but they already had too much on their plate with a raucous eight-year-old in the house, so she'd talked them out of the idea without any difficulty. Besides, she loved her house and didn't want to be away from her usual creature comforts, cushy goose down bed, sunny kitchen, and the fanciest Italian coffeemaker money could buy. Mac heard light footfalls in the hall and smiled, knowing Jordan was probably tiptoeing across the wood floors in deference to her need to rest. The house fell still. Mac closed her eyes and let sleep claim her.

It had been three days since Mac had traded her hospital bed for the comfort of home. Jordan hadn't officially worked all week, enjoying the time she was spending with her friend. This morning, like the two preceding, she entered Mac's room with a tray of breakfast goodies, and, unlike the days prior, Mac was still snoozing away.

This was unusual. Of the two of them, Mac had always been the early riser. Yet it was nine in the morning and she was still fast asleep. Jordan reflected back on many college mornings. Back then, she would lie in bed until the very last moment, while, no matter what had gone on the night before and for how long, Mac would be up at the first sign of light, ready to take on the day. All through med school and her residency, Jordan had preferred night shifts, always struggling with hours that required her to face the day well before she was ready.

Jordan smiled as she realized Mac must be feeling more comfortable with each passing day, a sure sign her injuries were healing. Jordan balanced the tray in one hand while trying to quietly rearrange the assortment of items on the nightstand to make room for the morning sustenance. Laptop, lamp, alarm clock, carafe of water, TV remote control, and a well-worn paperback. Finally, she picked up the paperback and moved to the love seat off to the side of the bed.

Mac's fascination with romance novels had been a source of amusement to Jordan throughout their long relationship. Mac had challenged her on several occasions, "Don't knock it 'til you've tried it," but Jordan always resisted the dare and kept to her own favorites in the nonfiction section. Relaxing into the chair, she decided it wouldn't kill her to see what all the fuss was about.

She'd been reading for a couple of hours when Mac stirred and pointed at the book in her hand. "Are you enjoying it?"

"Oh, this?" Jordan set the novel down on the bed. "I was moving stuff off your nightstand. Sorry."

"No worries. As long as you didn't lose my place."

Jordan leaned down and gave her a light kiss on the cheek. "Your dog-eared pages are safe with me. I'll be right back with your java, ma'am."

The rest of the week passed without incident. Mac's brothers took turns stopping by each evening with baskets of food sent, with love, from their wives. Nick sent platters filled with new creations he was trying out for the fall menu. Jordan commented she wasn't going to be able to leave the house because she'd eaten so much she could no longer fit through the doors. Despite the lame protests, she made no other mention of leaving. More and more of her belongings began to appear in the guest room, as she brought in a few new items every time she left the house to run an errand for her patient.

They fell into an easy pattern. Mac slept later than she had in the past and Jordan found it easier to get up and meet each day with the prospect of joining her friend for coffee as an enticement. Mac's rib cage was still painful, but her agility improved daily. This morning, in fact, she'd arrived in Jordan's room early and woke her with the aroma of fresh, hot coffee.

The endeavor, hampered by the healing collarbone, had taken three trips, but the sight that greeted Mac was well worth the trip. Gone was the dressed-to-kill Dr. Wagner with every hair in place. The woman in the guest room bore no resemblance to her dandy counterpart. Jordan lay sprawled across the bed, sheets and comforter tangled into knots. Her auburn hair was as rumpled as the sheets. One bare leg dangled off the bed and her torso was twisted in the opposite direction. Like Mac, she was dressed in worn flannel boxers and a threadbare T-shirt from her college days. Amazingly, she looked as beautiful in her boxers as she did in Armani.

Mac took advantage of the time before the smell of coffee woke her friend. She'd never noticed how relaxed Jordan seemed while sleeping. Maybe she never was when they lived together. Back then, she was completely preoccupied with making sure every waking moment was a step along the path to becoming a surgeon. Jordan had worked harder than anyone she knew while in school. Mac was sure her hard work had the dual purpose of blocking her past while ensuring her future.

Mac started to reconsider her plan. It had been over two weeks since their fight. With the intervention of the accident, she and Jordan had yet to discuss what had happened between them. In fact, they both acted as if nothing had happened, falling back into an easy friendship. Mac woke this morning focused on talking to Jordan about the night of her party and putting the incident behind them once and for all.

Pulled by the scent of fresh coffee, Jordan finally began to stir. Opening one blurry hazel eye, she croaked, "Is that coffee I smell?"

"You must be dreaming."

"You're right. I must be dreaming if the one-armed patient who's supposed to be taking it easy is bringing me coffee in bed."

"Oops. I was hoping you wouldn't notice." Mac smiled down at her sleepy friend. "But if I waited for you to get coffee, I might have bed sores."

Jordan sat up, pulling the covers over her bare legs. "Whatever. A little extra sleep would do you good. I'm a doctor, I should know." Noticing the serious expression on her friend's face, she asked, "Honey, what's up? Are you in pain? Do we need to take you to the hospital?"

"No, no. Physically, I feel fine."

"Well, something's wrong."

"I want to talk about our fight."

"Oh, yeah, that. I was wondering when the topic would come up."

"We both said some pretty ugly things to each other." Mac hesitated. "I'm not sure what happened with Rebeca, but I do know I don't ever want another woman to come between us. Our friendship is too important to risk."

"I couldn't agree more. I'm not sure which one of us she considered a win, but Rebeca is a player. She was definitely out to get something, and I'm sorry I reacted the way I did. I wasn't in a very good place when I stumbled on you two."

"Grace told me about her and your father."

"Yeah, I didn't know the half of it." Jordan relayed Grace's account of her mother's affair and its effect on her father. "I guess the important thing is he's happy now. He and I still have a lot to work out. I imagine we've both changed a lot since we were last speaking. In the meantime, if he and Grace are happy, who am I to interfere?"

"Sometimes happiness comes from surprising places," Mac observed.

Jordan looked into her friend's open, honest, brown eyes and thought no truer words had ever been spoken. In that moment, she was hit by the raw force of all the thoughts and feelings she'd held at bay. Happiness was right in front of her and though the source was surprising, the surprise was exhilarating. Adrenaline pushed her to say, "Mac, I've got a surprise of my own."

"You do, huh?" Mac responded idly, fiddling with the coffee creamer.

Jordan could tell she didn't appreciate the import of the announcement she was about to hear. She decided to take advantage of the theme of the day and surprise Mac with both the message and delivery of what she had to say. Reaching across the nightstand, she stilled Mac's hand and softly said, "I'm in love with you, Mackenzie Lewis. I've been in love with you for years."

She lightly touched her lips to Mac's. The moment their lips met, she knew her announcement was not only unexpected, but awkward. Seconds spent in the embrace only confirmed the knowledge, and Jordan drew back quickly. Seeing the unsettled look on Mac's face, she scrambled to her feet, desperate to distance herself from the increasingly uncomfortable silence. She walked quickly to the door, hoping her car keys were still on the kitchen table.

Tossing a quick "I'll check on you later" over her shoulder, she fled, unable to bear additional contact with the open wound of her newly professed feelings.

Blocks away, encased in the safety of her sedan, she called her father. Barely waiting for him to register the surprise he must be feeling at receiving the first phone call from his daughter in years, she plunged on. "I have some things I need to take care of and won't be able to stay with Mac for the next few days. Would you mind stopping by her house and checking on her?"

A brief pause followed, then she relaxed as he agreed to do whatever needed to be done. Jordan imagined he would bring Grace with him. She shuddered at the anticipation of the lecture she would receive once Grace found out she had abandoned Mac in an attempt to salvage her pride. Speeding home, she concluded preserving her pride was worth all her efforts. She would lick her wounds in private.

What the hell happened? Mac hadn't moved since Jordan had practically run out the door. *Jordan Wagner kissed me,* she mused dreamily, still tingling from the touch of her lips. Slowly swimming back to reality, Mac struggled to wrap her mind around Jordan's message. *She told me she loves me—no, she told me she's in love with me. And I sat here like a bump on a log.* No wonder she took off.

Determined to deal with the situation directly, she picked up the phone and called Aimee. "I need a lift."

Mac had an access key to Jordan's loft, but she forgot to pick it up as she hurried out of the house twenty minutes later. Even if she had, she didn't think it would have been good to barge in with it under the circumstances.

"Are you sure you want me to drop you off?" Aimee looked concerned. "I can come up with you."

Mac was thankful Aimee hadn't asked a lot of questions when she asked for the ride to Jordan's loft. She didn't have the energy to deal with explanations, though she was sure Aimee was wildly curious to know what prompted the request. "Thanks, but Jordan's taking me home. She wanted me to come over so she could check out my arm. She was coming from the opposite direction and I told her I could get a ride here."

Mac winced at the hastily hung-together lie, knowing Aimee couldn't possibly be fooled by the inconsistent story.

"All right, but if you need me, call me on my cell and I'll come get you." Aimee paused. "Mac, I love you."

"I love you too, Aimee. I'm fine. I promise."

Mac got out of the car and waited impatiently for Jordan to respond to her call on the intercom. The greeting was less than charming.

"What the hell are you doing here?" Jordan asked.

"Be mad at me if you want, but at least invite me up and be mad at me in person."

The buzz of the door lock was the only response. Jordan was waiting at the door to her loft and she waved Mac in, but didn't invite her any farther than the entry. She repeated her question, "What the hell are you doing here?"

"I wanted to see you."

"You shouldn't be driving until your arm heals, especially not a stick shift."

"I got a ride. I wanted to see you." Mac emphasized the last point with pleading eyes.

Jordan looked away. "I don't think you do. At least not the way I want you to see me."

Mac could hear the hurt and anger in Jordan's voice, and once again, she realized how big a gesture the kiss had been. She hadn't had time to process her own feelings, but right now she was focused on the disposition of the woman standing before her. Reaching out, she grasped Jordan's hand in her own. "Let me ask you something. Was this morning when you first thought you might have these feelings for me?"

Jordan appeared to be looking inside for an answer. After a moment, she responded, "No. I've felt this way for a while, but I first started to think I might be falling in love with you the week of Jeremy's party."

"Was your realization sudden or did it kind of creep up on you?"

"Kind of snuck up on me," Jordan admitted.

"So, you've had a little time to think about it?" Mac watched and waited. Jordan was smart enough to get her point and Mac was sure she would get it quickly. She wasn't disappointed.

"You must think I'm crazy. I declare I'm in love with you, and then run like a rabbit when you don't instantly respond in kind."

"I don't think you're crazy. Maybe a little feverish." Mac smiled, hoping Jordan was feeling resilient enough to enjoy a little levity.

Jordan grinned. "Maybe a little." Fastening an earnest look on her face, she asked, "Any chance I could interest you in a little fever as well?"

Mac's laugh faded into a blush as she realized Jordan's humor hid a serious question. Questions of her own flooded her mind. Was Jordan in love with her? Could she, did she feel the same way? How would her answer affect their friendship, the most important and longest lasting friendship she'd ever enjoyed?

A ringing phone interrupted her thoughts.

Jordan glanced at the caller ID and swore. "It's my dad. I

asked him to check on you. Chances are he's at your house and is wondering where the hell you are." She lifted the receiver and spoke into the phone. "Don't worry. She came over here to pick up some CDs. I'll make sure she gets back shortly We're good for the rest of the week. Thanks for checking. I owe you."

"Jordan, why was your dad checking on me?"

"I thought after the way you reacted to my declaration, you wouldn't want to see me anytime soon. And, frankly, I was pretty embarrassed."

Mac hugged Jordan close. "I'm the last person you should ever be embarrassed with. I love you with all my heart. Your little announcement surprised me. I still haven't had time to process how I feel about it, but my first reaction was to run to you, not away. Can you at least take that as a good sign?"

Jordan nodded.

"And can you give me a little time to think about how I feel?"

"Yes, of course." Jordan paused. "What should we do in the meantime?"

"Look, I know it's not fair to keep you hanging, but I need a few days to think. Okay?" She was finding it hard to look into Jordan's imploring eyes, knowing she had the power, but didn't yet possess the resolve, to grant her best friend's wish. "Meantime, I think we should go on a date."

"A date?" Jordan almost slapped herself in the head. All those years of school and she could only speak in one-syllable words. Mac must think she'd turned into a blithering idiot.

"You know, those occasions where two people meet and attend dinner or the theater and get to know each other over the course of a few hours."

"I think a date is a great idea." Well, at least she could speak in complete sentences.

"Great, Saturday night. Why don't you pick me up at seven?"

"Perfect." At this point, Jordan only trusted herself with small words and phrases. She allowed herself a silent ditty. *I have a date with Mackenzie, I have a date with Mackenzie!*

CHAPTER NINETEEN

"Y̶ou didn't have to ring the doorbell, you know." Mac waved her guest in, unable to keep her eyes from the small, tasteful bouquet of flowers in Jordan's grasp.

Following her gaze, Jordan offered the bouquet. "These are for you. And, frankly it didn't seem very date-like to use my key."

"Well, I suppose I need to be the good hostess then and offer my date a drink while I finish the last touches of my look for the night."

Jordan's gaze swept over her and her low whistle gave her considered opinion about Mac's look for the evening. Slim-fitting black slacks hugged Mac's well-toned legs, and a crisp sleeveless white shirt offset the light sling she still wore for her healing collarbone.

"If you think you can improve on what I'm seeing right now, feel free, Mac. But I don't think it's possible. How about I help myself to a drink while you take care of whatever you think needs doing? There's no need for us to pretend as if we've never been to each other's houses."

Mac, blushing from Jordan's compliment, seized on the opportunity to catch her breath in the other room while Jordan rifled through the bar.

"Would it be very rude for me to drink the last of your good Scotch on our first date?" Jordan called.

"A little, but if you hide the bottle in the back, I'm not likely to notice for a while." Ignoring her fast-beating heart, Mac dabbed on a light coppery lip color and took one last look in the mirror before she grabbed her purse, slung it over her good shoulder, and went to the living room to rescue the last of her Scotch.

"Are you starving," Jordan asked, "or would you mind if we made a quick stop before dinner?"

"Not starving, just some low rumbles from the beast within. What did you have in mind?"

"I swear it won't take long and then I promise you a great dinner. I made a reservation at Abacus."

"Fantastic. I promise I won't turn dinner into a review."

"I picked it because of their tasting menu. Don't worry. You'll get the full experience without having to order one of everything."

Mac grinned as she realized how comfortable it was to be with someone who knew her so well. Moments later, though, her grin turned sour as she realized they were pulling into a reserved spot in front of Sue Ellen's. Maybe Jordan didn't know her so well after all. "Jordan, what are we doing here?"

"Quick stop. I promise. Please come inside with me for a few minutes."

Very romantic, Mac thought grumpily. She got all dressed up to go into a smoky bar. It was barely even eight o'clock and she needed to be ten years younger and slightly buzzed to feel like she belonged here. A quick look at the wistful pleading in Jordan's eyes stopped the procession of thoughts and Mac forced herself from the car.

"This isn't what I envisioned for our date," she said as she slipped her hand into Jordan's.

It was too early for a cover charge. Once inside, Jordan led her to one of the tables near the bar. Mac couldn't help but notice the attention Jordan attracted from the assortment of women waiting for service. Despite the crowd, the tomboyish bartender skipped over the waiting patrons and hurried over to Jordan, leaning in to learn what her latest customer desired. Watching the exchange, the subtle way the bartender angled closer while offering returning whispers to Jordan, Mac felt jealousy churning her insides. Had Jordan seriously brought her to a bar to watch her flirt with other women? The bartender placed two Coronas in front of Jordan and waved off her attempt to pay before ducking out from under the bar and heading back to the deejay booth. Mac quickly averted her eyes as Jordan approached their table. She had no desire to let her see any trace of the jealousy she was sure was etched in the lines on her face.

Jordan held on to both beers and asked Mac to follow her out onto the patio. They sat in wire mesh chairs. Unable to restrain herself any longer, Mac opened her mouth to let loose with some fierce questions about why they were spending their first date at a bar.

Jordan beat her to the punch, asking, "Do you remember the first time we came here?"

Caught off guard by the question, Mac paused, casting back through some long-forgotten memories. "I sure do." Holding up her beer, she said, "Corona was all we drank back then, but we had to sweet-talk some of the older dykes at the bar into buying them for us."

Jordan smiled. "That's right. Do you remember the first time, though?"

Something in the wistful look on her face made Mac dig deep for the memory. As the remembrance washed over her, she blushed. She had kissed Jordan right here on this patio, hours after they had ditched their homecoming dates, changed clothes, and sneaked out to the bar.

"Ah, I think you're remembering now."

Mac expected another teasing grin, but instead she was met with an intense gaze. Jordan's eyes flashed with the spark of desire and she leaned in close. "Mac, can we try that kiss one more time?"

Mac answered with wordless lips. The first press of soft flesh came with a flood of memories, real and imagined. The first and, before now, only lover's kiss they had shared had been accompanied by surges of want and desire. Shortly after, she'd dwelt on the feelings their first touch had evoked, longing for more. Then came the sadness of unrequited desire. With time, the feelings had faded and she'd adjusted to the idea that she and Jordan would never be more than friends. Since then, she'd resolved to find those feelings with someone else.

But she never had.

She'd come close, but the range and depth of feeling was never quite the same. As she kissed Jordan now, she felt as if their ardor was all encompassing. Nothing could keep them apart. Their fast friendship, previously a limiting force, would only serve to make their love invincible.

The break in the newfound closeness was abrupt. Mac glanced up and caught Jordan grinning down at her. It wasn't a teasing grin, but a purely happy one. Mac smiled back. As they stood staring at each other, she caught the notes of the song playing and her grin grew wider. The deejay was spinning eighties tunes, and this particular one brought up memories. Though Whitney Houston was more likely to be heard crooning in one of the boy bars down the street, Mac recalled every deejay in town had been spinning her tunes when Whitney was in her heyday. "How Will I Know" was certainly appropriate background music for her first real date with Jordan, and Mac found herself mouthing the words.

"This song was playing the first time you kissed me," Jordan said.

Mac stopped tracing the lyrics and stared at her, marveling at the revelation. "It was?" she asked, mentally kicking herself for the inane reply.

Grinning, Jordan answered, "Yes. I remember everything about that night. How you looked, what you said, how it felt to kiss you. I didn't know then what I know now."

"What do you know now?"

"I know I can trust my feelings."

"And what are your feelings telling you right now?"

"That, once again, we're going to miss dinner at Abacus."

Jordan's loft was closer. She drove quickly, her ability to navigate impeded only by the urgent caresses of her frisky passenger. As they rode the private elevator to the penthouse loft, Jordan murmured soft thanks against Mac's lips, grateful the lift was reserved for her use alone. She had no idea how long they remained in the car, writhing with want and need, before finally Mac grasped her hand and led her into the loft.

Jordan glanced quickly around. Mac caught her eye and smiled. "Looking to make sure you hung up your clothes?"

Sheepishly, Jordan replied, "Dear, you know me well enough to know I would never leave clothes lying around. Actually, I was thinking my place seems kind of cold and uninviting compared to yours."

Mac's eyes swept the room and settled back on her.

Drawing Jordan close with her good arm, she spoke softly. "Your place is perfectly you. Sleek, solid, gorgeous. It represents all the great facets of who you are. I wouldn't change a thing."

Jordan melted. "It could be a bit warmer, though."

Pulling Jordan closer, Mac traced her lips with her own, delving deeper until their tongues were dancing with desire. She slid her hand under Jordan's shirt and palmed her back before moving slowly to her front. Resting her hand on Jordan's bare breast, she stroked her already erect nipple and looked her straight in the eye. "I'd say it's getting quite a bit warmer in here, don't you think?" At Jordan's nod, she added, "How about you show me to the bed and we'll see what we can do to warm it up too."

Jordan, realizing she was no longer in control of the situation, obligingly followed Mac's instruction and led her to the platform bed in the corner of the room. She'd counted on tonight being the first of several "dates," a series of events where she would court Mac and convince her to fall in love. She had no idea Mac, who focused so much attention on romance, would wind up in her bed on their first date. Temptation warred with a cautious voice within, and Jordan held still the hand unbuttoning her shirt. "Mac?"

"Yes?" Mac didn't look up from where she was planting gentle kisses along Jordan's neck and earlobe.

"Hey, Mac, look at me." Dreamy eyes glanced up at her and Jordan resisted the urge to lose herself in the promise of pleasure they delivered. "We don't have to do this tonight. I mean, if you're not ready, we can wait. I want our first time to be as romantic as your favorite love story."

"Oh, honey, there isn't a love story I've read that's more romantic than this."

Jordan's surprise was genuine. "You don't feel like having sex with me on our first date is decidedly unromantic?"

"Jordan, what we're about to do isn't having sex, it's making love, which wouldn't happen on most first dates. I think, in our own way, we've been dating most of our lives, waiting this long to be truly intimate with each other?"

Jordan grinned. "Wow, when you put it that way, we're long overdue."

"Ah, the Jordan I know and love. Now, take off your clothes and prepared to be ravished. I have quite a large collection of erotica mixed in with the romance novels and I've been waiting to try out some new moves on the right person."

Pulling her shirt off, Jordan said, "I'm developing a new fondness for your book collection."

"Consider this a private reading." Sitting directly across from her, Mac traced her lips up Jordan's bare abdomen, licking her way to her taut and ready breasts. Circling one nipple with flicks of her searching tongue, she stroked the other to aching erectness. Jordan's back arched as she thrust her chest willingly into Mac's loving embrace. With her arms around Mac's back, she loosened the sling and gently removed Mac's shirt. Urging her back down on the bed, she lowered herself until the tips of their breasts lightly grazed one another. Holding herself above Mac, she moved from side to side, reveling in the way the gentle caress of the barest touch ignited sparks of pleasure between them.

"Closer, come closer," Mac urged.

"Have to be careful, dear. Your ribs are healing."

Mac gasped. "Jordan, I want to feel you against me. I could come right now."

"Oh no, you don't. I want to feel our first time."

Jordan leaned across the bed and grabbed a silk-covered

pillow. Propping it under Mac's head, she lowered herself slightly to kiss her swollen lips. Mac locked onto her, pulling her closer, writhing beneath her, struggling for release. Gently detaching herself, Jordan motioned her intentions and received a hazy smile signaling assent. Turning, she settled her legs on either side of Mac's pillowed head and lowered herself into her lover's musky scent. Softly she traced Mac's inner thighs, enjoying the accompanying shocks and spasms she elicited with her tongue. Soon she felt her own thighs twitching from pleasure shocks and it became hard to tell whether the source of the titillation was the touch she gave or received.

Basking in the power of their combined caress, they shifted attention to each other's cores in synchronicity. Their strokes moved lightly at first, then with forceful measure as their tongues teased then kneaded. As their pleasure and passion mingled, the sum of the whole became too much for either to contain. Their bucking bodies welcomed release while each woman struggled to hold on for a moment more, lost in the intimate touch craved for so long.

Release eventually won out and they surrendered to the swath of pleasure cutting through their veins. Releasing cries of consummated craving, they climaxed together.

❖

"What day is it?"

Mac opened one eye at a time and turned her head toward the sound of the voice beside her. It appeared the words came from nothing more than a bundle of tousled red hair resting on the pillow beside her. Beaming as she reflected on the night before, she answered, "Pick a day, any day. It's a good one."

The rumpled red hair came to life as Jordan sat up and stretched a greeting to the sun shining in the floor-to-ceiling windows lining her loft. Reaching for a switch on her nightstand, she commanded the blinds to close.

Mac grunted. "Hey, what did you do that for? It's a beautiful sunny day outside."

Leaning down to kiss Mac good morning, Jordan replied, "Honey, don't you think we gave enough of a show last night?"

"A little like closing the barn door after the horse's been stolen."

"Only one free show for the crowd. I have plans for you this morning and I have no desire to share them with anyone who might be pleasure-seeking outside these windows."

"Fair enough." Mac returned her kiss. "Back to my original question, what day is it?"

"It's Sunday, dear. Why, you have a hot date?"

"I absolutely have a hot date and I'm in bed with her now." Mac snuggled in close to Jordan's naked body, enjoying the warmth of her lover's touch and dreading the information she was about to relay. "I invited the gang to brunch today."

"Gee, I haven't been to the grocery in days. I haven't a clue what we'll serve."

Mac poked Jordan in the side. "You know I meant the restaurant, silly. They'll be there at eleven."

Checking the bedside clock, Jordan said, "It's ten now. If you call now, you can probably catch them before they head out." Catching the look on Mac's face, she paused. "Ah, you want to go, don't you?"

"A little."

"You aren't feeling strange about last night, are you?"

Mac, puzzled at first, quickly realized she needed to explain lest Jordan jump to the wrong conclusions. Drawing her close, she whispered, "I feel lots of things about last night—loved, satisfied, and excited, among others. Strange isn't on the list.

As much as I don't want to put on clothes and share this time with anyone else, I want to go. Partly because I promised them I would be there, but mostly because I want them to know about us, unless you don't want them to know."

Jordan's laugh conveyed her relief at knowing Mac didn't regret their newfound intimacy. "You will not rest until you flush my reputation as a playgirl. I should have known you were out to get me from the start."

Mac smacked her with a pillow. "I don't think you need to worry about your reputation. You can still be a playgirl, but all your playing will be with me. If last night is any indication, you have enough play in you to keep us frisky for a lifetime."

"Don't you forget it. Now, if we're going to make brunch, we better hustle." Jordan stood at the edge of the bed giving her a wicked smile. "We only have one hour and one shower."

"Well, Mac, I guess you won't have as much need for the romance in these pages anymore." Haley picked up a book from the collection under Mac's chair.

Jordan interrupted Mac's response with a question. "You know, while you were laid up, I started reading the novel you've been reading. What's it called?"

"*Lost Lives, Lost Loves.*"

"Right. Well, I must say it didn't seem very romantic to me. Great lovemaking scenes, but it seemed like the two main characters weren't going to stay together. Irreconcilable differences."

"They'll get together," Mac said confidently.

"Seriously, I don't think so."

"They'll not only get together, they'll live happily ever after."

Jordan shook her head. "I don't see it."

"Honey, it's a romance. The main characters always get together. If they didn't, it wouldn't be a romance."

"It's that easy?"

"Oh, it's not always easy, but it's always inevitable."

"Wanna be main characters with me?" Jordan asked with a grin.

Mac smiled. "Oh, sweetheart, we've been each other's main characters for a very long time."

"Then I guess we all know how this story ends," Jordan concluded. She punctuated the remark with a passionate kiss.

As their lips sealed the promise of love, Mac stared into her best friend's eyes and saw the woman she'd been looking for all along. Her future wife.

About the Author

Carsen Taite is an avid reader and writer of lesbian fiction. Carsen works by day (and sometimes night) as a criminal defense attorney in Dallas, Texas. Though her day job is often stranger than fiction, she can't seem to get enough, and her goal as an author is to spin tales with plot lines as interesting as the true, but often unbelievable, stories she encounters in her law practice.

Carsen is married (Canadian-style) and she and her spouse live near White Rock Lake in Dallas, where they enjoy cycling and walking the trails with their fuzzy beasts.

Her upcoming titles include *It Should Be a Crime*, coming from BSB in 2009. For info check www.carsentaite.com.